ent★urage™

a lifestyle is a terrible thing to waste

Written by Tim Swanson   Designed by Ph.D

Published by Pocket Books
New York London Toronto Sydney

Produced by Melcher Media

IT'S NOT TV IT'S HBO™

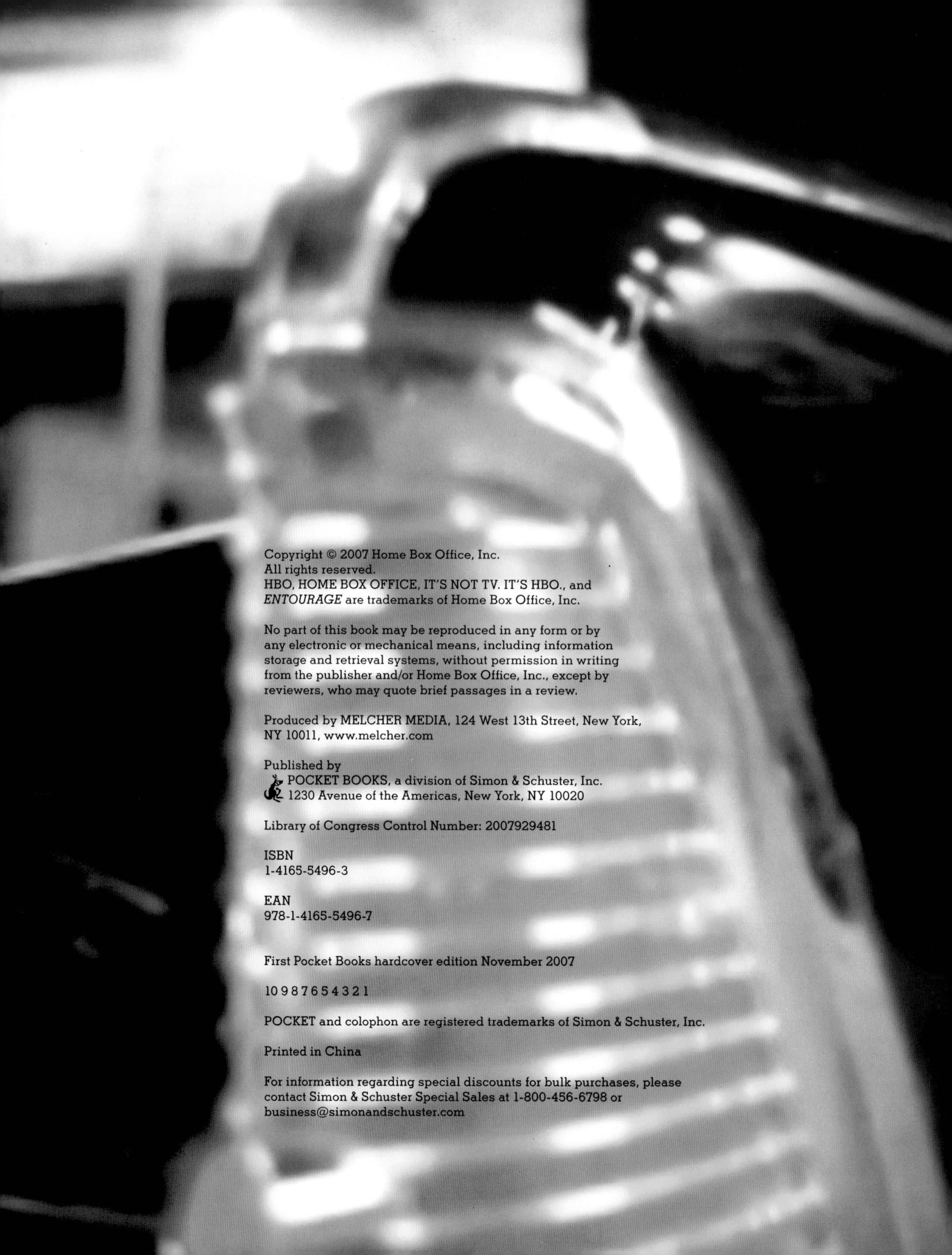

Produced by MELCHER MEDIA, 124 West 13th Street, New York,
NY 10011, www.melcher.com

Published by
POCKET BOOKS, a division of Simon & Schuster, Inc.
1230 Avenue of the Americas, New York, NY 10020

Library of Congress Control Number: 2007929481

ISBN
1-4165-5496-3

EAN
978-1-4165-5496-7

First Pocket Books hardcover edition November 2007

10 9 8 7 6 5 4 3 2 1

POCKET and colophon are registered trademarks of Simon & Schuster, Inc.

Printed in China

For information regarding special discounts for bulk purchases, please
contact Simon & Schuster Special Sales at 1-800-456-6798 or
business@simonandschuster.com

CONTENTS

ENTOURAGE HOTSPOTS: EAT, DRINK, LIVE THE LIFESTYLE

pg. 158

⍟ **CHAPTER 1**

victory
how it all got started ›››

Before "Turtle" there was Donkey. Before the character of "E" there were two real-life inspirations: a cool-headed confidante who also went by the single-letter moniker and a trusted, longtime manager. There was also John Alves, a.k.a. "Johnny Drama," the chef-slash-actor who served as the crew's spiritual guide. And, of course, before "Vincent Chase" there was Mark Wahlberg, the Boston-raised rapper who became an A-list actor, making a name for himself in films such as *The Basketball Diaries*, *Boogie Nights*, and *The Perfect Storm*. Back in 2001, the guys were struck with a simple, yet stunning, idea. Why not make a TV show about themselves hanging out and living the high life in Hollywood? They could base it on their own entourage: charismatic characters looking for success—friends that kept the actor grounded while he was pursuing fame and fortune. Wahlberg's manager, Stephen "Lev" Levinson, took it to his college buddy, a young and talented stand-up comedian and writer/director named Doug Ellin. What they ended up with has become a pop-culture phenomenon, a hit show that not only offers a VIP pass into the intoxicating and often absurdly hilarious world of celebrity, but one that also imparts a deeper message—that true friendship can, in fact, conquer all.

Mark Wahlberg: How did this thing get started? Everybody's got their own story. That's the funny thing about it, you know? Lev has been working with me since day one. He was my agent's assistant when I first started acting. Then he became my manager. And he's been with me ever since.

Stephen Levinson: Mark and I have been working together for a long time, and we used to go on the road for business and travel internationally when Mark had to promote his movies. It would be me, Mark, Eric Weinstein, Johnny Drama; Donkey would come, too. Funny things always used to hap-pen to us, and we would say, "Wouldn't it be funny if we had a camera and turned it into a show?" So E and Mark and I would always joke about that. And then one day, it just kind of popped into our heads: "We should really do this as a fictionalized show for HBO."

MW: I always had a crazy group of guys around me. I mean, people from everywhere, all ages. Sometimes you just want to hang out with your friends. You're get-ting to experience all kinds of crazy stuff, so you certainly want to share it with them. Everybody was just fascinated by them because it was crazy.

It was hilarious, you know? Random, bizarre shit going on all the time. We had been kicking around some ideas for a show, and we were very interested in getting into television. And Lev knew Doug; they were good friends, and I knew how talented Doug was.

Doug Ellin: I'm from Long Island, New York. I came out to Los Angeles after graduating from Tulane University and worked in the mailroom at New Line Cinema. I made a couple of independent films and wrote a bunch of scripts that didn't get made. Fortunately, Lev also went to Tulane, and he and Mark had this idea and came to me and said, "*Entourage*. Mark and his friends in Hollywood." And I said, "I don't really get it. Why would I want to see a bunch of guys living off another guy?" And Lev said, "Why don't you just do it and you'll figure out how to do it the way you want to do it?" He has done that a lot in my life, pushed me into things that I figure out along the way. Lev's a very big-picture guy. I'm more of a small-detail guy, so it's a good balance.

MW: When we first started talking about the idea, people thought it sounded like a reality show, but that wasn't what we wanted to do. I certainly didn't want to be putting my own business out there.

SL: Doug's strengths are character, dialogue, and comedy. He has a diverse skill set that goes beyond just writing. Since we had worked on *Kissing a Fool* together, I knew he was an accomplished filmmaker. We certainly had a dream that went beyond just having a script developed. We hoped that we could beat the odds and actually make a show, because it's such a long shot to get a show made.

DE: Their initial idea was just Mark and his boys. I needed to find some way to make it something I could really understand. So I came in and said, "They've got to be like a family. These guys have to have grown up together, known each other from way back when." And then we went from there. When I came on, I asked Mark if they could be New York guys, because I didn't know anything about Boston.

MW: I didn't care if they were from Boston or not. All that mattered, you know, was getting the right characters that really clicked well together. I didn't care if they were

from Ohio. As long as they had that family thing together, you know what I mean? With my family, when I was growing up, there was a lot of tough love. The way we grew up, we always would mix it up a little bit. I'd fight with my brothers and my sisters. That's how we settled a lot of disputes.

DE: I knew Mark from Lev. We were more acquaintances than friends, but I had met his guys. I looked at Mark and his friends—E, Donkey, Johnny Drama—basically as models, like, "Let's take a movie star and let's take these character traits from his friends." More than anything about Mark's actual guys, I was obsessed with the name "Johnny Drama." I had to have it on the show. So the real Johnny Drama, who I love and I know very well—he's a great guy—some things are taken from him, but a lot of things are taken from friends of mine, and it's just a mix and match of stuff.

MW: Johnny Drama, I call him my cousin. He's from Plymouth, Massachusetts, but I met him out here in Los Angeles. My brother hired him to keep me out of trouble; this was like when I got out of jail. He was basically, you know, babysitting me while I had to go back to court over and over and over again. Johnny Drama was one of the big reasons why I became an actor. Believe me, back then, I had no interest in acting.

DE: The character of E came from Lev, but obviously Lev and Mark didn't grow up together. Lev was a young assistant; nobody believed he knew what he was doing, but Mark believed in him, so they rose up together. E's also based on Mark's old friend, Eric Weinstein. Honestly, when we started, there were about eleven characters in the entourage and we slowly whittled them down. With three guys, everybody had a purpose. From minute one, we were like, "Let's be as realistic as possible. Let's not overexaggerate it. Let's find the funny in what actually goes on in Hollywood instead of

Creator Doug Ellin and Executive Producer Stephen Levinson strategize with director Julian Farino (from left to right).

taking it to a level that isn't accurate." Because the best movies and shows are the ones that make you say, "That's me and my friends," when you see them.

MW: Doug's a really talented guy. I mean, you immediately felt like these guys were really from a neighborhood—that they grew up together. He knows this world. When we went in, it seemed like it was going to be one thing; and then when we came out, it was guys from Queens.

DE: So at this point, we have the concept, and Lev and I are sitting around going, "OK, what should we do? Should we come up with a whole treatment? Should we write a script on spec? What should we do?" We always wanted this to be an HBO show. It was HBO or bust. So we sat down for dinner with Mark's agent, Ari Emmanuel, and said, "We've got this idea for a show called *Entourage*." He listened and then he goes, "We're going to HBO tomorrow." We went into HBO and honestly, I didn't say a word. Ari said, "It's *Entourage*," and then he said, "Doug will write it. If it's not good, we'll get someone to rewrite it." That's what he said right in front of me.

SL: Ari wasn't Doug's agent at the time, but the pitch was comical, as you can imagine. We sold it based on our experiences. It was more about what the story was going to be, not really anything we had done yet with the execution.

DE: The way I originally wrote the pilot, they're sitting in a limo after the premiere, and it's gone really badly. I mean, the movie sucks and nobody knows how to tell him. And that was what I thought was interesting. How do you tell a movie star his movie's a disaster? To make matters worse, he's running out of money. They're living a ridiculous lifestyle, and everything is crashing.

We wrote the pilot, and Steve, Mark, and I thought it was awesome, you know? When I handed in that script, I was a hundred percent sure we were getting it shot. And I will never forget, I was sitting on my bed and had my baby son in my hands, and Lev called me. He's like, "They don't like it." I'm like, "What don't they like about it?" And he said, "Everything."

SL: Doug said, "Really?" I said, "Yeah." And that was that. He asked what we were going to do now. I said, "I think we're going to go in and talk about it."

HBO President Carolyn Strauss: When we first started developing the script, Doug had a very, I would say, gritty idea of what this show was. I think it was just like a bunch of knuckleheads with money. Truthfully, what we saw was the opportunity to have a lot more fun with it. In our conversations with Doug, which he responded to incredibly well, we talked about having more fun with the characters and with the situations and really taking advantage of that sort of fantasy element of what the show was.

DE: In that meeting with them, they're like, "We still feel there's a show here." At that moment, I'm wondering, Are they going to get another writer? Am I out of this thing? What happens now? I went off to

Palm Springs for a week and wrote a completely different script with a different tone. The note that they kept giving was, "Fun. We just want it to have more wish fulfillment."

CS: Putting this show together was a process, like anything else, and Doug just rose to the occasion every step of the way. We knew there was definitely something in there that was going to work.

DE: It's not that the story was so different in the earlier version. It was the tone that was different. It was much darker. I'm not sure why I was inclined to go that way. In the rewrite, the guys had a great premiere. There are hot girls all over the place. And they have a big agent who's telling them they have a big movie that's available to them. It's all wish fulfillment. You want to be Vince in that one. You don't want to be Vince, the down-and-out movie star whose life is over before he's thirty. It was definitely the smarter way to go. HBO committed to seven episodes after the pilot. We didn't have any of the rest of the season planned. No arc. Nothing. So after we did the pilot, it was like, "OK, what's next?"

> "It's all wish fulfillment . . . it was definitely the smarter way to go." DOUG ELLIN

The Real
Johnny Drama

How did you meet Mark Wahlberg?

I met Mark through his brother, Donnie. Donnie ended up being the best man at my wedding. We've been together since Donnie and I were probably eighteen and Mark was going on seventeen, during the New Kids on the Block era. Back in the day. How it all started, my cousin was a bodyguard for the New Kids, and that's how I met Donnie. We immediately hit it off. We were like brothers. And later on he said, "My brother's in jail right now. Would you be willing to go home and help him when he gets out?" Meaning back to Massachusetts. I was in Los Angeles then, acting. I got a couple of commercials, you know, a Gatorade commercial and stuff like that. I had done the ABC series *Coach*. But when I found out only ten percent of actors actually work and then only three percent can pay their bills, I had to get on a hustle, you know what I mean? So Donnie hired me to keep an eye on Mark—he was just getting out of the Plymouth House of Correction. It was almost like the good Lord had everything in store for us, because when he got out of the Plymouth, I took Mark down to my mother's house there, and he was like, "I know your mother." I'm like, "How do you know my mother?" He said, "I met her in the jail." My mom goes and talks to the prisoners about the Lord.

How did you help him out?

I called myself the big brother. I think Donnie only paid me three or four hundred dollars a week. Back in the early '80s, I was making $1200 a week, so it was kind of humiliating. I did all Mark's cooking. I did all his cleaning, the whole nine yards. I used to do all the laundry. We'd come off the road, and I'd be home with two or three hockey duffle bags full of dirty clothes. I did everything. When he first started making big money, it was just like, "I'm done, you understand? This is done." I told him, "Bring in the professionals." But now it's more like, "Hey cousin, let's take a walk on Wilshire and play eighteen holes." The chores have turned around. I've been reaping a lot more benefits now that we're not struggling as we were back in the day.

How did you get the nickname "Johnny Drama"?

It was, God rest his soul, from one of my best friends that passed away from cancer last year, Keith Naughton. We used to call him "Kizzy." With acting, I had what I called the David Caruso theory. I'd get these small parts that were like one line, and so I'd make the most of them. And he'd say, "Man, you were unbelievable. You've got nothing but drama." And I used to say, "That's right, bro. I am drama." So he started calling me Johnny Drama.

How true is the character of Johnny Drama to who you are in real life?

Well, man, if you've seen me, I'm 6'2", 190, ripped up, with green eyes. So all of that shit about banging these big body-building girls or me looking at guys' calves—it's great writing is what it is, you know what I'm saying? Because none of my girls ever looked like that, including my wife. But Kevin Dillon, I love what he does. He's funny. I give it to him. He's got all his chops as far as acting. But to compare him to me would be an injustice because, you know, I'm more spiritual. But the cooking? Absolutely, brother. I cook. Real deal cooking with Johnny Drama.

11

→ ERIC WEINSTEIN:

The Real E

I was born in Manhattan and raised in the Bronx. In 1971 I was seventeen and working at the greatest clothing store in the world: Granny Takes a Trip, the store where all the rock stars bought their clothes. There I met Alice Cooper, and started to help him out. Eventually, I became a roadie, touring with bands like Blue Oyster Cult, Kiss, Black Oak Arkansas, The Dictators, Shakin Street, and then Patti Smith. I met Jim Carroll through Patti Smith and Alan Lanier. Jim had a band called The Jim Carroll Band, and he wrote the book *The Basketball Diaries*. ¶ In 1981, my mom passed away, and I went on this run of heroin. There were not enough drugs in the world to kill the pain. By 1984, I had gone through all the money I could con, and I was on my last legs. I had been evicted from an apartment when I couldn't pay rent—and it was only $250 a month. I was putting every nickel in my arm, from cocaine to heroin. I was also addicted to Methadone, and after hitting rock bottom I found this program on the Lower East Side. It's a great, great program, and I ended up walking in there homeless and walking out of there the program's director.

Eric Weinstein (left), Johnny Alves, and Mark Wahlberg appeared together in the *Entourage* pilot.

¶ One Wednesday night, I was working late and I got a call: "We have a kid that we want to hire for a part in the movie *Basketball Diaries*, but he doesn't know how to act like a heroin addict. Can you help him out?" The actor, James Madio, got the part the next day. Then the producer, Liz Heller, asked if I would meet with Leonardo DiCaprio and the film's director, Scott Kalvert. They loved me—we got along great because I knew Jim Carroll and the whole story. Once I started working with Leo, they said, "Well, would you mind working with Mark Wahlberg?" And I said, "No, not at all." So I ended up working with everybody when it came to the heroin. ¶ Meantime, Mark was just starting his acting career. *Basketball Diaries* was his second movie, and I told him I believed in him. I thought one day he would be a great actor, because he was so real and true to himself. He was just starting to put together a team. He didn't have anybody else. And you know, I was older, single, and I had road experience. There was nothing holding me back. He asked me if I wanted to come to Europe with him. He had an album out called *Life in the Streets* with Prince Ital Joe. He was very big in Germany. So I went to Europe with him in August of '94. After that, we came back and he asked if I would come to his next gig. However, he didn't have any money to pay me. I think my first paying job was the movie *Fear*. I got $300 a week. I was driving him, taking care of whatever he needed. If anyone wanted him, they'd call me. It was just like being a road manager. ¶ Then some of Mark's older friends from his neighborhood would try to come around, try to hang out and work, but they never really could get it. They would end up staying for half a movie, then get fired. It was hysterical. The entourage itself was really hysterical. For instance, one of the inspirations for the character Turtle is this guy named Donkey. He had a great, great heart. And Johnny Drama—Johnny Alves—would always be around looking for a part, looking to better himself and his career. He is the spiritual inspiration the entourage needed. He'd never be on set with us a whole movie. He'd do some great cooking and show up at lunchtime, and then you would find him on the golf course or in the gym. The rest of the entourage was usually spending every waking moment trying to con someone out of something or convince cute extras that if she slept with them it would better her career. ¶ Anything these guys were doing, any scams they were up to, they would get busted because they weren't that good at it. We'd be on set and I'd catch one guy going into the trailer and saying, "Oh, Mark wants two cases of water, two cases of iced tea and, by the way, can you get six cases of Bud Light?" At some point, I said, "Fuck it, I'm buying a camera and I'm going to start taping everything these guys do." Lev would call up every day and I'd tell him everything that went on. "You wouldn't believe what happened today. You wouldn't believe what happened yesterday." ¶ Women always say things like, "Are you really like that?" Or they go, "How do you deal with Drama and Turtle? In real life, don't those guys make you crazy?" I say, "Yeah, they make me fucking nuts." At five o'clock in the morning, they'd be like, "Yo, E, I messed up. The car got towed," or, "Yo, E, so-and-so disappeared in Vegas." So they drive you nuts. But you get used to it. And underneath it all, it's a crazy kind of love, the dysfunctional family type of love. We scream and yell at each other sometimes, and we also make each other laugh our asses off. All in all, if I were in a jam, there is no one else I would want in my corner but this entourage.

Doug Ellin, Rob Weiss, and Stephen Levinson are often giving shout-outs to people and places from back home in New York. Left, Lev's beloved Eddie's Pizza in New Hyde Park, New York: "We need an Eddie's in L.A.," Vince moans in one episode.

➔ MARVIN ELLIN

Doug Ellin's Father

and the real Marvin the Accountant

I never miss an episode, and I never miss calling Doug right after it airs. I know what Doug's old friends are like, and I see them in effect being portrayed on the show. For instance, the name Scott Siegal, that's his closest friend in real life. The way Doug portrayed him is nothing like how Scott Siegal really is. Some of the other characters have different names, but you could tell that they were based on his friends growing up, how they were and what they were like. He depicts Marvin the accountant to be a little like me. Some of the things he says I say: "You've got to stop spending. You've got to save. You can't do this kind of thing." The character doesn't look like me and doesn't act like me, but everybody took Marvin the accountant to be me—all my friends, all my clients. As I told Doug, it's cost me a lot of money. When I go down to Florida, I wear the *Entourage* hat, and when the caddies and the valets see it, they go crazy and ask about the show. They tell me it's their favorite show, so I can't give a buck anymore when they return the car. I've got to give five bucks.

> **A FAMILY AFFAIR!** Lucas Ellin (Doug Ellin's son), left, plays Jonah Gold on the show, while his grandfather, Marvin, inspires the character of Marvin the Accountant.

behind the scenes

Doug Ellin (Creator and Executive Producer) // I've got three or four people I really count on, people I can spitball ideas with, like [writer and producer] Rob Weiss. He's one of the funniest guys I know, and as soon as the show got picked up, I knew he'd be perfect for it. He directed a movie in the early '90s called *Amongst Friends*, which played at Sundance, and the Billy Walsh character on our show is based on Rob. So that should tell you all you need to know about the guy.

Rob Weiss (Executive Producer) // I've known Doug since the tenth grade, and we've remained friends out here. And I've known Lev since he was an assistant at UTA. He was the first person to see any footage of *Amongst Friends*. I know Mark Wahlberg from Mickey Rourke. When I first moved out to L.A., there was a whole scene of guys from the East Coast that used to go up to Rourke's boxing gym, so I met Mark and most of Mark's crew there, like the real Johnny Drama and all those guys.

At the beginning with the writers, it was just Doug and Larry Charles and then me. Here's basically how it works: We look at what the season's arc is going to be, depending on the episodes, and we pick big moments that will get to this place. Then it's sitting around a table and throwing out funny shit, just loosely tossing the ideas around. And then we start honing in, actually breaking down that episode and picking the big moments to build to in the end. If the goal is to get *Aquaman*, and Vince is like, "I'm in and I want to do it," then the episode ends on a high note. The next episode, there's a problem with getting it, because James Cameron doesn't know who he is, so you're ending on a low. You want to vary the highs and lows.

David Frankel (Director) // I honestly didn't know what to make of the *Entourage* pilot script. It was very funny, and it depicted a familiar world from a surprising point of view. You just wanted to feel like you were there, like you were part of the entourage. But the guys, Doug and Lev, had a clear vision for the show from the beginning. My first day in the office, they showed me tapes of the actors they wanted: Jerry, Kevin Dillon, and Adrian. I thought Jerry was too young, Kevin was too old, and Adrian didn't seem at all like Mark Wahlberg, our fearless leader, who was the inspiration for Vince. But when we got them all together in a room, they were authentic and very funny. Connolly needed persuading. It was a tough part—in the pilot, Eric had the biggest role but the least definition—but somehow Lev persuaded him to audition. The minute he opened his mouth, it sounded like Doug had written the part for him, and he just got sucked right in. In the end, his energy and heart helped define *Entourage*. For all its honesty and cynicism about Hollywood, for all its voyeurism and thrill-seeking, it's really a sweet show, a love story about the friendship between these five guys. And it's hard to go wrong with a great love story.

Julian Farino (Director) // There's a sort of anarchy to directing *Entourage*, which I think is a really good thing for the show. It's very loose; very humorous. It's not the most disciplined set, you know, but that's the spirit of it. The whole skill to directing *Entourage* is about capturing the energy. It's a show that needs to play at a high pitch, a high level of energy, and if that drops, the material suffers badly, in my opinion. So we try to create the right atmosphere so that everyone pretty much enjoys it. And the way in which I go about shooting the show is really to facilitate that. You try and capture it rather than stage it, so it's not too slavish with coverage, because then we'd all get bored shooting the same thing 50 million times. I try and let a lot of things happen in the frame, so that all the guys are forced to play off each other in that way that gives you the heart of the show—it's about friendship and loyalty, and the more that you feel these guys have got a secondhand nature, the better the material plays invisibly. So that's the principle.

An ordinary day on the *Entourage* set: From left, executive producer Rob Weiss with Dennis Hopper; Adrian Grenier and Stephen Levinson on the beach in Malibu. Below, Doug Ellin, on location in Park City, takes a break from shooting Season 2's "The Sundance Kids."

Episode 1: **Pilot**

> **Airdate: July 18, 2004** | **Directed by David Frankel** | **Written by Doug Ellin**

Vincent Chase is a movie star. His new action movie, *Head On,* just premiered, women are salivating at the sight of him, and Hollywood is buzzing. The entourage kills it at the premiere party—and an even better after-party—but the next morning, it's back to business. Trying to cash in on the Vince Chase buzz, Ari pushes Vince to do the Disneyland-set popcorn flick *Matterhorn*, but Vince and E agree to turn it down.
> Director David Frankel was nominated for an Emmy for this episode.

16

Episode 2: **The Review**

> **Airdate: July 25, 2004** | **Directed by Julian Farino** | **Written by Doug Ellin**

Ari has an axiom: "You always book your next job before this one comes out." Unfortunately, Eric and Vince didn't adhere to it. Now, in the face of *Daily Variety*'s scathing review of *Head On*, the heat Vince was generating a week ago could suddenly disappear with a few more critical bashings. This, however, isn't enough to stop Vince from sinking $320K into a new Rolls Royce Phantom. Or heading out to Jessica Alba's house to party with a hot pop star. While E worries about Vince's career prospects, Drama worries about his next acting class assignment, performing a piece from *The Vagina Monologues*.

Ari → "I resent this. I don't have dinner with people like you. I don't do it. I don't do this. Do you think Hugh Jackman calls me up and goes, 'Hey Ari, listen, love the script, but I gotta run it past the pizza boy.'"

Episode 3: **Talk Show**

▶ Airdate: August 1, 2004 | Directed by Julian Farino | Written by Larry Charles

Johnny Drama's no newcomer to Hollywood. Back in the day, Drama and Jimmy Kimmel were tight, but when Jimmy went off and became a big talk-show host, Drama's phone calls were no longer getting returned. With Vince booked on *The Jimmy Kimmel Show* to promote *Head On*, Drama sees it as a chance to confront his former friend. Vince scores an encore with former one-night stand, and fellow Kimmel guest, Sara Foster. And Turtle, never one to shun an opportunity, negotiates a free home theater for the Chase mansion. All he's gotta do is get Vince to plug "Home Theater Solutions" on the show.

Episode 4: **Date Night**

▶ Airdate: August 8, 2004 | Directed by Daniel Attias | Written by Doug Ellin & Rob Weiss

Eric's got a thing for Ari's cute new assistant, Emily, who asks him out the night of the *Head On* premiere. But first dates can be tricky, especially when your best friend turns it into a group date. While Vince secures pop star Justine Chapin as his date, and Drama brings his new girlfriend/workout partner Tanya, Turtle picks his date out of Vince's fan mail and winds up with a scorching hot, but utterly crazy, obsessive Vince fan. Ari spends the night sweating out whether his client's flick has what it takes to hold off a "Pixar Squirrel" at the box office. ▶ Perrey Reeves was shuttled over directly from filming her last scene in *Mr. and Mrs. Smith* to play Ari's wife.

Episode 5: **The Script and the Sherpa**

▶ **Airdate: August 15, 2004** | **Directed by Adam Bernstein** | **Written by Doug Ellin & Stephen Levinson**

It's not every day a naked guy comes up to you and hands you your dream project, but that's exactly what happens to E when he receives the *Queens Boulevard* script from Ari's old assistant and rival, Josh Weinstein, in the locker room of Gold's Gym. With L.A. suffering through the most severe marijuana drought in years, the guys are miserable. Luckily, Vince's new vegan girlfriend, Fiona, knows a Sherpa who lives in Bel Air and grows his own weed. The pot hookup proves to be very fortuitous for the guys when they meet with *QB* producer Scott Wick that night.

Episode 6: **Busey and the Beach**

❯ **Airdate: August 22, 2004** | **Directed by Julian Farino** | **Written by Doug Ellin & Larry Charles**

After *Head On* scores big at the box office, Ari presents the guys with a bevy of high-concept, big-money offers, but *Queens Boulevard* is the only project E and Vince want to do. When Josh Weinstein tells E that Ari is dragging his feet on the *QB* deal, E threatens to relieve Ari of his agenting duties. With the guys at Weinstein's beach house for a party, Ari "storms the beaches of Malibu" to take down his rival and reclaim his client. Down on the beach, Turtle has to endure Gary Busey's strange idea of retribution, after his clumsy mishap taints Busey's art show. ❯ Though Busey didn't actually paint the circle-centric painting, "Emotional Dyslexia" (below), in his fictional art exhibit, the painting now hangs in the entryway of his home.

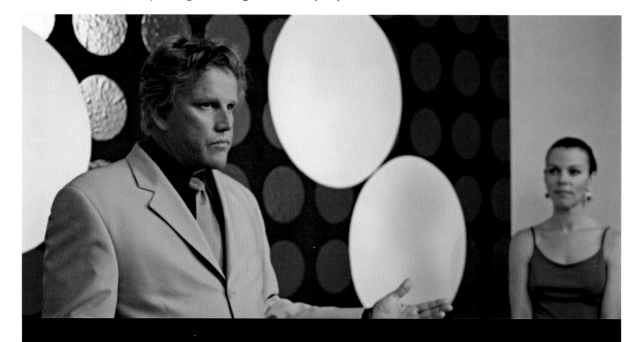

Gary Busey →

"This piece evokes all of the emotions from what I call a discombobulated man. This is emotional dyslexia. This is emotional confusion. Now, what is emotional confusion, you ask? It's like running naked through a cornfield backwards at midnight."

Episode 7: **The Scene**

▶ Airdate: August 29, 2004 | Directed by David Frankel | Written by Rob Weiss

Over lap dances with *Queens Boulevard* writer/director Billy Walsh, Vince commits to star in Walsh's film. The following day, Vince has second thoughts due to a guy-on-guy scene written into the script. While E and Vince debate the merits of working with a great filmmaker versus playing gay on screen, Turtle lines up strippers to come to Vince's private screening of Walsh's first film, *Days*. Vince, blown away by *Days*, decides to trust Walsh and take the role. Walsh reveals that the gay scene was in there just to test Vince's trust in Walsh and was never meant to be shot. ▶ When producers were looking for a "wacky, big-mouthed East Coast indie filmmaker," they looked no further than the episode's writer, Weiss, who helmed the 1993 Sundance fave, *Amongst Friends*, to play himself. But Weiss passed, giving birth to Billy Walsh, who is played by Rhys Coiro.

Episode 8: **New York**

▶ Airdate: September 12, 2004 | Directed by Julian Farino | Written by Doug Ellin & Larry Charles

As the guys get ready to leave for New York to shoot *Queens Boulevard*, Eric looks to make the leap from "glorified gopher" to Vince's manager. While Vince makes house calls to all of his L.A. girls, Drama auditions for *CSI: Minneapolis*—and bombs. Although Turtle's planned a going-away party for Vince, the discontent in the group due to E's position has them in no mood to celebrate. Prepared to go to New York without E, Vince, Turtle, and Drama hop on a private plane, but Eric shows up on the tarmac just in time to get a commitment from Vince that he's now his official manager.

★ CHAPTER 2

riding the jet stream

the boys >>>

vince

Adrian Grenier

Manhattan–bred actor/filmmaker/musician Adrian Grenier was "slumming it" down in Mexico's Yucatán Peninsula trying to pick up some Spanish when he received the call from his manager, Stephen Levinson, about auditioning for the role of an almost-famous movie star for an HBO pilot. But just like the talented, principled, and just-slightly-aloof character that he would soon play, Grenier wasn't overly eager to jump at just any project, and left the suits hanging for a while. "I was doing my own thing," he says, laughing. He eventually answered Hollywood's siren call—or at least Lev's frantic e-mails—and now he's glad he did. "This show is amazing," he says. "I mean, we basically get paid to have fun all day long, to enjoy ourselves, to indulge. I can't imagine why I wouldn't have wanted to have this exact job all along."

At first, you weren't interested in the part of Vince. Why not?
I wasn't entirely interested in the project because, initially, I thought it was a little superficial. But I've learned a lot about enjoying myself more since *Entourage*. The show has actually taught me how to laugh and enjoy life in a way that I never could before.

You made yourself hard to cast. What was that about?
I didn't make myself too available for much auditioning. I kind of came in at the end, and I think that worked to my advantage because whenever you see actors come in and be vulnerable in a room, suddenly, they lose that sort of celebrity mystique. Even the biggest stars will bomb an audition. But because I refused to subject myself to that, I was almost larger than life in the eyes of a lot of the people casting, because I made myself more mysterious. And I think that intrigued them. I feel like I gave them the character. I didn't try to "act" the character—I was the guy.

How are you and Vince alike?
Like Vince, I'm not going to jump for any opportunity, you know? I'm very content where I am and have a secure sense of self. I think that's important for this character, because despite all of the influences of the business, he still manages to maintain a certain groundedness. But, in general, I'm a lot more low-key and down-to-earth.

In the earlier versions of the pilot, you didn't see Vince a lot. But you helped to make him a more central character.
I sort of insisted. I said, "Look, I don't want to play just a pretty face, I want to be in the show. I don't want to

just be this guy who's just sort of there, you know? I want to be in the show. I also expressed that I thought they were overthinking the whole notion of celebrity. They built it up too much. He's not trying to be cooler than anyone else. He's just one of the guys. The show's not about Hollywood. It's not about making a lot of money. It's about friendship, period. So after talking to Doug [Ellin], when I finally did come out for a meeting, we worked on a happy medium.

What's up with Vince's game with the ladies? He seems like he's getting less play these days.
Apparently, he doesn't have any game anymore. E's got all the game. E gets the threesomes. He's getting all the play these past couple seasons. I don't know what happened. I mean, Vince is established. Vince has nothing to prove. He's getting his fair share. The first season or two, every other day I'd walk on to the set and there would be a new girl that I had to do a scene with. And then since the first two seasons, I don't have any scenes with girls anymore. But you don't have to see Vince succeeding with the ladies. You know he is. We want to see if E can actually succeed with the ladies.

When the four of you go out together in real life, are you competing for women?
We've never really had that problem. I think there was maybe two seconds during the first season when we were all single, and then it got pretty ugly. But we all have completely different taste in women. And Kevin Dillon is married now. So he's no competition.

Do you still go out to the clubs?
Yeah. Occasionally. Sure. When I'm really lonely [laughs].

What's it like working with the guys?
It's amazing. All the guys are so down-to-earth and so unaffected. All of us guys are just totally appreciative of our position and of each other's company. I show up and I'm on set all day long doing what's expected of me and laughing the whole time. These guys, whether we're doing a scene or not doing a scene, there's just such a good, happy, content feeling. And everyone feels the same way. Although Kevin Dillon always said (in Drama voice), "I'm going to teach you how to play golf, man. I'm going to teach you how to play golf." And I was like, "OK, big brother." He never taught me how to play golf! I'm friends with the guys. I always say that Kevin Connolly was miscast. He should have been Vince.

He's more like Vince. He knows everyone in Hollywood. He goes to clubs, flies in private jets. See, I'm acting when I play Vince. I'm actually more like E.

How is your character related—in your mind—to Drama?
It's funny because every once in a while, we'll come across a scene where our history is relevant. I'll have my own back story created and prepared and I'll come in and Kevin Dillon and I will start talking about it. I'll be like, "Yeah, well, you know, we have the same father." And Kevin will be like, "No we don't. We have a different father. We have the same mother." I'm like, "No, no, we have the same father. I don't know, in my mind we do." And we have this big debate and, of course, we have to open it up to a larger conversation with Doug Ellin and the other guys.

Wahlberg on Grenier

Adrian, as you know, is very different than me. But the essence is there. And like Vince, when I actually started working and doing some things, I had my people doing jobs, you know? You got your friends and people that you trust. Why not?

What has this show done for your career?
I've definitely experienced an escalation of celebrity in my life in the past few years because of *Entourage*, but even to this day, I'm not as famous as Vince is. I would say that I'm a B-actor playing an A-list celebrity. And I've actually been very lucky to have Vince as sort of a dry run at celebrity, you know? I get a sense of what I would endure and what I would avoid at all costs. And it's helped me to pace my own entrance into celebrity. Celebrities are just regular people. They're just their own selves. That's why they are celebrities, because they don't conform to anybody. They're exactly who they want to be.

Vince often seems troubled by the price of fame. Are you?
I think a lot more so than Vince. Vince embraces every opportunity that he's given and truly appreciates it, and I think he may seem nonchalant and like he doesn't care about what people think. But I think his biggest struggle is that deep down inside, he does have a huge burden of having to live this life of a celebrity, which is not easy. I see Vince as really scared at times, you know? Of course, it's a comedy and we're not going to delve into those dark corners of his soul, but I know from experience that being in the public eye is not easy. And also to have to endure the pressures of criticism and of warrantless appreciation at times—those are the prices that you pay when you become a celebrity.

How true is *Entourage* to the Hollywood you've experienced?
When I read the first episode of *Entourage*, I thought it was a little over-the-top. It was a little unrealistic, and I rolled my eyes and said, "OK, that's stretching it." And then I started doing the show and started tasting a little bit of the Hollywood life. And I was floored because I realized that it's actually less exaggerated and actually a bit underplayed. It cuts things out from what actually happens in Hollywood, because if you put all that stuff in, people would say, "Oh that's just ridiculous." So you know, it's more realistic than I would hope.

You play drums in a band called The Honey Brothers. Are your bandmates like your real-life entourage?
No. I've been with them for five years. And an entourage is more associated with celebrity. It's just a fancy way of saying friends. And yes, I have friends. I'm not a complete loser. But you know, I don't think that Vince would say he has an entourage. He would say, "These guys are my friends. These are my boys. We are all equal."

Why does Vince love the *Medellin* project so much?
I think it appeals to the rough-and-tumble parts of Vince and his friends, reminds him of his old life in Queens that was a little less dainty than it is here in Hollywood. There's definitely an appeal to outlaws who represent rebellion against structure. I think that's sexy for everyone, even if they are criminals. There's a mystique about them that Vince likes.

There's been talk of making a real *Aquaman* movie, or a *Ramones* film, and there's even a real script for a Pablo Escobar/*Medellin* story. Do you have interest in starring in any of those films?
People ask me all the time whether or not I'm going to play Pablo Escobar in real life, or Aquaman. Am I going to do *The Ramones*? I would, of course. I mean, it's fun, you know? Making those movies is a lot of fun and I love filmmaking and I love acting, so I would do it. But the idea of becoming more famous than I am is scary. And the idea of becoming as famous as Vince is quite scary.

ON TREATING A CELEBRITY:
A Hollywood Expert Analyzes the Star

"Maybe you can have it all" is an *Entourage* slogan, but is it really possible for all the boys from Queens to have every one of their desires fulfilled? When it comes to fame and friendship, it's no secret that one can often eclipse the other. Orville Gilbert Brim, noted social psychologist and author of the upcoming book *The Fame Motive*, says, "If you become famous, you need to protect yourself from all kinds of events, whether physical or financial or social. And this buttons up friendships because there are things you experience that you can't convey." But if Vince manages to climb to the top, will it bring him happiness? Brim says that the characters' motivations are a clue to their futures. Vince and Drama may want to be famous movie stars, while Eric and Turtle might just be after the good life—money, power, and women. In the long run, that means Eric and Turtle have a greater chance at true happiness, since fame rarely provides the satisfaction that spotlight chasers think it will. "All the evidence shows that the two brothers, regardless of their media fame, will never be satisfied," Brim says. "The higher you go, the more you want. Fame is not an answer to the unfulfilled desire for approval and acceptance. It only seems like it. So it doesn't really make you happier in the end, because you are always trying for more and it never fulfills this basic need."

Lucky Brand Jeans, an old T-shirt, a Just Cavalli striped shirt, and a pair of boots give Vince his hot style.

30

An Armani shirt and Gucci pants paired with Converse are perfect for a night on the town without looking like you're trying too hard.

THE MOVIE STAR WATCH: A Chanel J12 Superleggera

○ Sunglasses make the LA man: the Penguin Belize SLUs

The equally stylish Modern Amusements for daytime—or night ○

"For Season 4, I'm trying to keep his colors a bit more subdued," explains costume designer Amy Westcott. "I'm going for the anti-contrived look for him. He doesn't need a lot of work to make him look good. The idea behind him is that he's not very thought out. Vince is supposed to roll out of bed and look amazing because he throws on some designer pants (he wears Gucci pants all the time), sneakers, and a rock-and-roll T-shirt—like the Cult—and he's ready. He doesn't need to think about it.

"Some of the shirts I buy from thrift stores, and we also work with many companies like Trunk and Worn Free. Trunk is a brand that makes old concert shirt replicas, like an old Dead Kennedys shirt, but it's new. It's worn out so it looks like it's been in his closet for a while.

"I like the whole military thing on him, but I use a lot of different styles as far as jackets go, from classic army jackets to pea coats. I also like button-down shirts for Vince. Part of his look includes extra-long sleeves and open cuffs to stay a little haphazard."

○ Let the ten-percenters carry the BlackBerrys. Vince uses the Samsung phone.

Vince's women

① **Ali Larter** → We're not exactly sure what went on between Vince and the actress Drama calls "Illegally Blond," but we can assume it ended badly: E asks Turtle to make sure that she's not sitting "within ten rows" of Vince at the *Head On* premiere.

② **Bikini Girl on Raft** → According to Turtle, after each premiere, Vince likes to go night swimming, and the younger Chase brother ends up having a wet and wild night with this female fan.

③ **Chick in Blue Dress** → A small mention on Vince's romantic résumé that reminds us about the limitless perks of being young, rich, talented, good-looking, and famous.

④ **Sara Foster** → After a "crazy night in the Hamptons," Vince never called the *Big Bounce* actress, but the two reconnect in her dressing room and then announce that they "had sex five minutes ago" when appearing together holding hands on *The Jimmy Kimmel Show*.

⑤ **Justine Chapin** → The pop singer takes a break from her "Pure Tour" to go on a group date with Vince, who tells her that he doesn't want to work for her physical affections. Big mistake. "I would have given you the best head you've ever had," she says.

⑥ **Fiona the Vegan** → Even E gets a glimpse of how stunning this yoga-toned tree-hugger looks in the buff. But can holding off sex really be part of a cruelty-free lifestyle?

⑦ **Carol, the White-Tank-Top Girl** → She may be just one of many, but at least Vince can remember her dog's name, which is Philly, his "favorite terrier."

⑧ **Reverse Cowgirl** → Vince proves that he's more than just a missionary man with this insatiable hottie who moans, "I've never been with anyone who can fuck this long." Vince's reply? "I've been training for a movie." Spoken like a true actor.

⑨ **Janeen, the Juice Box Girl** → This bubbly brunette picks up a post-coital Vince on Wilshire Boulevard after a frustrated E leaves him stranded. The two end up enjoying some time in the "jacuz" back at the mansion.

⑩ **Jaime Pressly** → What started as an agreement to do a telethon for canine MS ends as a dual-celebrity fling with the two actors kicking up sand at Pressly's beach house.

⑪ **Madam Staci** → Vince didn't even know his new squeeze was pulling a Heidi Fleiss until Bob Saget broke it down for him. But at least Staci's generous with her employees, insisting that her girls take care of Turtle and Drama free of charge.

⑫ **Li Lei** → Actress Bai Ling, as a martial arts master, teaches Vince the tricks of the trade with a simple verbal instruction: "If you want to be hot as iron, you first must master laying horse stance."

⑬ **Mandy Moore** → This time around, it got even uglier than the *A Walk to Remember* incident. Vince may have slept with half the actresses in Hollywood, but the second go-round with Mandy nearly kills his professional career and his friendship with E.

34

⑪

⑫

⑬

⑥

⑭ **Sundance Publicists Corine and Jen** ⟶ Eric and Vince warm up in the hot tub on a chilly Park City night with corporate flacks Corine (the one who sends them cases of Budweiser every month) and Jen (the one who sent them the Maserati).

⑮ **Sienna, the Vodka Tonic and 25 Girl** ⟶ This hook-up goes down smoother than the drink she offers to buy Vince near the pool at the Roosevelt Hotel.

⑯ **Lindsay, the Cocktail Waitress** ⟶ A coatroom quickie at Sloan's charity event with this sexually adventurous student—who happens to be studying labor law—almost morphs into a weekend in Napa before Sloan and E decide to roll solo.

⑰ **Nicole, the Celebrity List Girl** Vince hooks up with this undercover bride-to-be at Book Soup and learns that he tops her fiancé-approved celebrity sex list after they engage in some afternoon delight. "These types of women definitely exist," says actress Lindsay Sloane, who played Nicole. "I mean, I don't think anyone ever thinks that they could actually land the famous people on their list, so it's more of a fantasy, which makes it OK for you to talk about with the person that you love. But every single one of my friends has a list. It's been the subject of dinner conversations numerous times."

⑱ **Amanda** ⟶ Sometimes the best way to diffuse sexual tension in a working relationship is to just engage in an energetic sex marathon, which is exactly what Vince does with his smart, sexy, and sophisticated agent. But mixing pleasure with business can be problematic, even in Hollywood, where the two often seem interchangeable.

⑲ **Samantha, the Malibu Girl** Vince hops in this girl's convertible on the PCH on the way up to Malibu to see her famous friend, Dennis Hopper. While Samantha is worried that Vince might be more interested in meeting the Easy Rider, Vince makes it clear that, at the end of the day, they'd be riding back to his place together.

⑳ **Juliette, the British Linen Girl** Although Vince is supposed to be helping E get laid, he isn't about to turn away this British beauty and owner of her own line of linens. However, while they're in her room, working in her customized sheets, E gets some alone time with her top sales rep, Heather.

㉑ **Monica, the Antique Desk Salesgirl** ⟶ While picking up an antique desk for E's new office, Vince doesn't hesitate to pick up the smoking-hot salesgirl as well.

㉒ **Lori from Bristol Farms** Part of Turtle's job has always been bringing hotties back to the mansion to party with, and he came through again with this girl he met in line at the grocery store.

35

⑤

⑱

⑯

⑭

eric

Kevin Connolly

When casting the role of best friend and manager Eric Murphy (a.k.a. "E"), the straight-shooting, sensitive-but-tough "every guy" who doubles as both the show's conscience and moral compass, the producers came up with a brief list of professional actors to audition. One of their top choices was Long Island native Kevin Connolly, who had made a name for himself in both TV and film. The only problem was that Connolly was taking a break from acting. "I was working as a director," he explains. "I was getting ready to do a movie called *Alpha Dog*, and I was in this crazy independent-movie director mode, so I was resistant to auditioning." It took a phone call from his old basketball buddy Mark Wahlberg to convince Connolly to come in to the *Entourage* offices for a sit-down. "Mark just called and said, 'Kevin, listen, I'm asking as a favor to me,'" Connolly says. "'Just explore it and go in and see.' I went in and read it and it just took off from there."

How do you know Mark Wahlberg?
I just know him from being out here in Los Angeles. Leo DiCaprio's a buddy of mine, and I met Wahlberg when they made *Basketball Diaries* in 1994, so it's been a while.

Was it surprising for you to get a phone call from him?
No, we're friends, so it wasn't like, "Oh God, why is he calling me?" I knew it was business. And he's such a good guy. If he calls you to come and sit down and ask you something, you do it because he would do it for you. He's just one of those guys.

Right. You guys play hoops together.
Yeah, we still play. It used to be we'd play my friends and me against his friends and him up on his court at his house. We played some high-tension games. Very competitive.

You had some previous experience with the show's subject matter. You were in a movie about an entourage called *Don's Plum* with Leonardo DiCaprio and Tobey Maguire. And you were once actually a part of Leo's crew, weren't you?

Here's the thing. We were all friends and Leo's career took off first, so it felt that way. I did a TV show with Tobey in '92 called *Great Scott!*, and that's how I met Leo. Tobey and I were roommates in the early '90s. But it was different from the show because we were all actors. *Entourage* is one guy and everybody is working for him. It was never that kind of a thing with us. We weren't out of work. It's like, you'd get a pilot, get paid forty grand, and then you lived on it for a year. Then Leo's career pops. Tobey pops. I get a sitcom. People just started popping. And so with Leo, they would want him to go to Europe to promote something and he wouldn't want to go, so they would tell him he could bring four or five friends to sort of lure him into going to do this stuff. Then all of a sudden, we're flying around in private jets. He just exploded. It happened overnight. It was so crazy.

How's your golf game these days?
Not very good. You should ask Kevin Dillon. You know, Kevin is a fantastic golfer. If you watch the show and you really break down everybody's swing, you can see that Kevin is the golfer of the bunch. Jerry's the worst, but he's apparently getting a little bit better. I remember one day, we were rehearsing a scene in front of the golf simulator and I hit a hole in one. The guy that was running the thing said he had been working for the company for fifteen years and had never seen it before. I'm looking at Kevin Dillon and all of a sudden, he looks pissed. He should be happy that I got a hole in one, but he's jealous. He's jealous that I got a hole in one. It's so funny. I said, "Are you jealous?" He's like, "Yeah, a little bit. A little bit."

It seems like you guys are pretty competitive with each other.
Especially at the golf simulator. People cutting through the game area almost get their heads taken off with a golf club. It's a healthy, competitive sort of thing. Everybody's really so different, but we are a tight bunch. It sounds like a cliché, but we really are a tight group of guys. I'll tell you, one night I was in a bar in New York and a guy comes up to me and is like, "Derek Jeter wants to know if you want to come over and have a drink with him." I'm like, "Yeah." Derek Jeter is probably the only guy in the world that I would get up and walk across the bar for. So I walk over and bullshit with him, just talking about the show, and he's busting my balls, and then he said, "Can I ask you a question? Do you

guys really all get along?" People want confirmation that we are as tight as we look. That's a common thing.

What do you remember about shooting the pilot?
You know, pilots are tricky. You're trying to establish characters. You're trying to do a lot. So I knew that the pilot was tricky. I've done so many pilots and you just never, ever, ever know. I was pleasantly surprised once we got going. The critics jumped all over the show and they loved it, which is a big help. It was nice, too, because I was ready to get crucified. But all of a sudden, everybody just loved the show.

How are you feeling about playing Eric these days?
At the end of Season 3, I'm finally the producer. Eric makes a bold move and uses his bank account, gets involved as a producer. In Season 4, I start my company, so I get my own office, taking on another client. My company is called the Murphy Group. You'll see a little turmoil between Vince and me. I think you may see Ari and E side up a little bit. There has to be some kind of evolution in the relationship between those two characters. It's like it can't be me threatening to beat Ari up every time he steps out of line. He can't faze me anymore. But look, I'm the whipping boy, the pizza boy. It's my job just to take it.

He is like Mr. Nice Guy to the point where he doesn't want to hurt anybody's feelings. We shot an episode about the fact that E cannot have emotionless sex. The guys are trying to get him to go and just bang a girl and not call her. And he's going, "Why would I do that? Why would I have sex with a girl, knowing that I'm not going to call?" But that's also Doug Ellin. Doug is the kind of guy who never wants to ever hurt anybody's feelings. E and Doug are a lot alike that way.

Have you ever eaten at Sbarro before?
Of course I have. And I take heat about E working at Sbarro all the time. I remember I was doing *Live with Regis and Kelly*. I was outside making a phone call before I went on, and some guys come up to me and they want me to sign Sbarro plates. And I said, "I'm going to sign a couple of these just because this is so ridiculous." It's funny, the whole pizza boy thing, you know?

How was the threesome scene with Emmanuelle Chriqui and Malin Akerman?
Awkward. Really awkward. For that particular scene, I had a girlfriend at the time. And Emmanuelle has a boyfriend. So there wasn't any sexual tension between us. Everybody was settled into his or her relationships, so that part of it was out of it. It was very professional. It was just a little awkward, especially since I don't have to take my clothes off and they do. So I'm fully clothed, trying my best to make them as comfortable as possible. But those sex scenes aren't that fun to shoot. The girl's got Band-Aids on her nipples, you're sitting there in your underwear, and there are people working around you. It's far from like, "Whoo! This is a good day at work."

Well, the good part is that E seems to get laid more than anyone on the show.
Adrian complains about that all the time. He's like, "I am the movie star. Why does he get all the girls? I don't understand." And I think it's because my character represents more of an everyman, and I think Doug sees himself as E a little bit, you know? It's funny, though. With the character of Sloan, I mean, is there a more perfect woman in the world? She does charity work and she's like, "Oh sure, let's have a threesome. Go out with your friends every night. Do whatever you want to do and come home and I'll be waiting for you. I'll cook for you." I'm like, "Doug, who is this woman?"

Have you met the guy your character is based on?
It's funny because the character of E, Eric Murphy, is really a cross between Eric Weinstein and Stephen Levinson. I'll give you an example. Leo [DiCaprio] was in Italy for nine months doing *Gangs of New York*. Some time later, Wahlberg is going there to do *The Italian Job*. All right? So Eric Weinstein calls Leo, gets him on the phone, finds out about all the cool clubs, the hotels, the restaurants. When Mark goes there to work, Friday night comes around and Weinstein already has a table at the best restaurant and knows the best club. He's ahead of the game. He really does run the show. He's a few steps ahead of everybody. Mark also takes very good care of his guys, too. It's not a bad business.

What do you think makes a good manager?
A good manager helps his client decide what movies to make. He makes the calls on projects. Every movie that Vincent Chase has done in the history of *Entourage*, E has signed off on, you know? Even *Head On*, that first movie in the pilot, he picked for him. E picked the script for *Queens Boulevard*. E convinced Vince to do *Aquaman*. He told him to pass on *Matterhorn*. A good manager has to be picky.

The show makes it seem like all celebrities know each other. Is that the reality?
There is something to that. You do find yourself in strange circles at times. I was at some party a while ago and I found myself standing in a circle with Suge Knight and Verne Troyer. I was sitting there thinking, OK, guys, this is weird. This is really weird. Verne Troyer's calling me E and I'm like, "Dude, that's not my name."

Do you have a favorite episode?
To this day my favorite episode of *Entourage* ever is "Sundance." All of a sudden, I got my boys from Long Island going, "I'm going to Sundance next year!" We gave people outside of Hollywood a look into what Sundance is really like. We did two-and-a-half pages of running dialogue while walking down Main Street. That was an accomplishment. We were the first people to do Sundance. It's just awesome, man, getting to shoot in all these different locations. And nobody's taking it for granted. We are very aware of the fact that we're doing something special. I'm not going to let one second of it go unappreciated. This is the greatest job ever. And there will never be another job like it.

ON CONSTANTLY HAVING TO DO DIALOGUE ON A CELL PHONE

It's a pain in the ass. The only person that talks on their cell phone more than me on TV is Kiefer Sutherland on *24*. I just use my own phone on the show because I'll get confused with this phone and that phone. It's just easier to use your real phone. I have a BlackBerry. It's the greatest thing in the whole world. It's my favorite. It's what I use and they keep a backup in case I leave it in my trailer or whatever, which is never.

A REAL MANAGER ON E

Stephen "Lev" Levinson, Executive Producer

How would you rate the job that E is doing for Vince as a manager?

I'd say E is doing a fantastic job. I think that E's motives are always pure, and he always has Vince's best interests at heart. Hollywood does not own E, and that's why he can make smart decisions for his client. E didn't arrive in town owing anybody any favors. He's his own man and so is Vince. If you go down the list of everybody around Vince—and this includes Ari—they've all got love for him but they have their own opinions and they're all brutally honest. That's what's really great about them. That's how Vince is able to stay grounded. They keep it real, and that gives you a chance of keeping your head on straight while figuring out all this Hollywood shit.

"His look has evolved the most over the past four seasons," says Westcott, the show's costume designer, about Eric. "We're giving him a dressier look because he's Vince's manager. Clothes that garner respect. This season, we have him in a lot of suits, dress shirts, and pants,

because he's going to meetings. We're assuming that he's got business to take care of.

"He has a very different color palette than Vince. I keep him in a lot of light blues, greens, and grays, and black and white. It's a bit more serious than the other guys' palettes. A bright shirt

would be out of character. I save the colorful clothing for Turtle and Drama.

"When it comes to jeans, I use a lot of good old-fashioned beat-up Levi's on E. He is a straightforward no-nonsense type.

For shoes, he's a big fan of the Nike Air Max 95. I actually get a

42

He may have just moved west, but the kid from Queens dresses perfectly California casual: C&C T-shirts, Levi's jeans, and Nike Air Max 95 sneakers.

Movin' on up: When E becomes Vince's manager, he upgrades with a Ralph Lauren khaki blazer, Paige Premium Denim Jeans, and John Varvatos black dress shoes.

lot of them custom-made through Nike.

"E would shop at Theory. But also Calvin Klein, Ralph Lauren—designers that specialize in clean lines. But we go out on a limb every once in a while. He has a Rufus shirt with fancy French cuffs, Elie Tahari button downs with front placket details, and we also go to John Varvatos for interesting sweaters. Certain designers just look really good on him."

Mosley Tribe Pilot
THE EFFECT: Make 'em forget "Pizza Boy."

Tarondo Crono Sport

Never, ever leave the house without a BlackBerry Pearl.

Becoming a producer means dressing for serious business: A Theory dress shirt, sweater, and dress pants with Armani shoes say, "I have arrived."

Sloan may be the privileged daughter of super-agent Terrance McQuewick, but she always comes across as one cool, down-to-earth chick; a good girl who would spend her days organizing charity events, but would still be up for a three-way with her blond best friend at night. Too good to be true? Maybe. But definitely too good to last.

Do you share any personality traits with Sloan?
Everyone on this show has something in common with his or her character, so there is a basis to begin with and then we just sort of build on it. That's part of the reason why the casting is so amazing.

What's she really like?
She's really well-to-do and she's just this cool, grounded chick who isn't about the Hollywood fluff. She was attracted to E, not Vince. Over time, their relationship just kept growing stronger and stronger. Doug, Kevin, and I spent a lot of time talking about it, wanting to keep the relationship special. And then it was just something that continued to grow and develop. Doug always said he wanted to keep her incredibly sophisticated and classy and just very intelligent and different from some of the other women who come and go on the show. Doug never wanted to cheapen Sloan in any capacity.

Except with her three-way with Kevin Connolly and Malin Akerman's characters.
Even with the three-way. I mean the night before, you know, Malin and I came to set, and we met with Doug. We had like a private sort of discussion/rehearsal. Kevin was there. It was incredibly laid out. It's like a dance. It has an absolute choreography, and if you don't know what you're doing, it just looks ridiculous. You don't leave it up to chance because it just comes off as so goofy. We discussed the scene a lot. We didn't want it to be gratuitous. We didn't want it to be like cheap and dirty. So really, on the day, it was like really easy-breezy. But we were all nervous. Everybody just wanted to bang it out.

No pun intended.
No pun intended. We get going and we do the first take, and Doug comes up to us and he's like, "OK, girls. It kind of looks like you've done this before." We're dancing all supersexy and we're like fully kissing and he's like, "Whoa." He wanted to make it really seem like this was the first time for Sloan and that she's nervous when she waves Eric over, which was such a cute moment that so many people responded to. For Malin and me, it wasn't actually so bad because we didn't know each other very well, so it was still very, you know, new. But like with Kev, it was so weird because we're friends. I do believe we all took a shot of tequila before shooting that scene.

45

Sloan and That Infamous Threesome

Nothing ruins a threesome experience
like waking up with feelings for the other woman.

Turtle and Drama's Threesome Experience

Turtle >	Me and Drama had a little incident.
Drama >	Don't fucking say it, man.
Turtle >	We accidentally crossed swords.
Vince >	Really? Were there any women there at least?
Turtle >	Yeah, dick, it was a threesome, OK. It's no biggie. Crossing is an occupational hazard.

drama →

Kevin Dillon

We might as well clear this up right off the bat. Doug Ellin did not base the character of Johnny Drama—with his hilariously tragicomic exploits and absurd opinions about basically everything—on Mark Wahlberg's older brother, Donnie (of New Kids on the Block fame). "I find it bizarre that people think that," Ellin says. "Donnie's a successful actor who is also a very wealthy guy." Nor did he model Drama on the man who plays him, Kevin Dillon (younger brother of Matt Dillon), who also boasts an enviable acting career in both film and television. So who's his muse? Drama is based, very loosely, on Mark Wahlberg's good pal John Alves, a.k.a. "Johnny Drama," a bodybuilder/spiritual guide/one-time TV actor and mainstay of Mark's real entourage. "The real Drama isn't like my character at all," Dillon says. "He's a much more down-to-earth, grounded guy. He's got a wife and kids. The writers know him, but Drama has become his own animal, with what they put in the scripts and how I play him."

What do you remember about auditioning for *Entourage*?
I had just finished a show on CBS called *That's Life* and I had some down time. I was looking for a job, auditioning, doing pilot season again, which I hate. They sent over sides for a new HBO show. And Johnny Drama, at that stage, wasn't much. It was just a couple of lines. I was like, "I can't do anything with this. It's too small." There's nothing worse than going into the audition with three lines. Auditioning is so stressful to begin with, and you just can't impress with a couple lines. So when I went in, they combined some of the other characters' lines and gave me those, so I was able to actually do something in the audition. When I went in, I saw Wahlberg, who I knew back in the day. We came really close to doing a movie together actually. It was a Mickey Rourke movie that neither of us ended up doing. It was good to see him in there. I did the audition, got a lot of laughs, and then came back and did it again. We did it probably about five times, maybe more. I think Jerry came in like twelve times or something. I actually saw Jerry at one of the auditions, too, and I bummed a cigarette off him. He was sitting there and he had his Knicks uniform on and a Yankees hat. I said, "Are you from New York?" And we started

talking about the New York thing a little bit. And that was still early on, so we still had a long way to go before the screen test. When we finally got to the screen test, I didn't realize that I wasn't up against anyone. They liked me so much that they didn't put anyone up for my character. But I had no idea, so I was looking around the room and there's about maybe forty-five guys there. I picked out a couple of the guys I thought I was up against and it turns out they were all up for different parts.

Are you like your character at all in real life?
Well, I'm not really like Johnny Drama. We have similarities as far as acting and up-and-down careers. So that's definitely something that's there. But everything else? Not really. I'm certainly not as obsessive as Johnny Drama. But I think that fans like to see his struggles. What it does is really show another side of Hollywood. Not everyone's going to be Vince. There's going to be Johnny Drama struggling out there as well. And as much as he struggles, he still works. He still gets jobs. He's got a nice résumé. When you think about it, Drama is a relatively successful actor. He's a good actor. So I don't play him as a bad actor. I play him as a good actor who's just unlucky. He works too much to not be good.

Do guys like Johnny Drama really exist in Hollywood?
Yeah, there are definitely guys like him out there. Drama's a very out-there character, but I know some guys who are similar. It might take about five guys combined to make a Johnny Drama because he's so complex. But there are guys whose egos go to their heads a bit, and a lot of it comes from insecurity. And Johnny Drama, with all his struggling, is insecure. His ego obviously gets in the way.

Can you cook as well as Drama?
No. But I'm not too bad. Every once in a while, I'll get into it. Do a nice soufflé. I like to make some nice crepes in the morning in a nice crepe pan.

How do you view Drama's past with the rest of the guys?
Drama's obviously the older brother, so he didn't really go to the high school with the other guys. He was graduating while they were maybe in junior high school. And that's one of the strange things, too, is the Turtle-Drama relationship. These guys are so close, but yet there's a big gap in age, you know? And then there's the size difference. It adds to the Abbott and Costello kind of feeling.

Did you ever think that your "Victory" battle cry would catch on the way it did? I never did. I just said the line and then later on, people started saying it all the time. As a matter of fact, we were recently working on Santa Monica Boulevard doing a club scene, and me and Jerry were sitting in the Cadillac and a guy walked by and went, "Hey Jerry, I love you, man!" Then he walked by and he saw me, he goes, "Hey, Johnny Drama! Victory!" And he did a great "victory" too. He held his hand up and everything. That happens a lot nowadays. It's very cool. It's just like Jeremy Piven saying, "Let's hug it out, bitch." All of a sudden, that became the catchphrase. It's pretty wild how that works.

49

What about playing Johnny Drama gives you joy?
I just love the character and all the different sides to him. He's got so many layers. And he's fun, you know? I can't wait to see the scripts because of the situations that they put Johnny Drama in. It gets me pretty excited just to read the scripts, but also I can't wait to see what kind of humiliation are they going to put Johnny Drama through this time.

You were injured pretty badly last year while shooting.
I broke my wrist. There's a plate and ten screws in there. In the middle of a shot, I landed on Adrian's foot while playing basketball at the mansion. I was coming down and I rolled my ankle over and that's what caused me to fall and the wrist snapped behind me. I hit the ground and I just knew it was broken. You could hear it snap. The crew was right there because we were shooting, and I guess you could see it on film. I've never seen it. I just said, "Get me a van. I got to go to Cedars-Sinai immediately." They said, "Let's get the medic up here." I said, "Just get a van up here." It was pretty ugly. My hand was kind of just hanging off to the side. Connolly actually had to run into the house. He couldn't bear to look at it. He was like, "Ohhhh…" The bone broke a little skin. It didn't totally come through, but it was almost a compound fracture. You could see where it was just kind of sticking out. Oh, it was ugly.

How long were you out of work?
That was a Friday, and then we ended up having to do a shoot on Sunday morning, so I went right from the hospital to do a photo shoot for *Entertainment Weekly* the next day and it was pretty crazy. And then I was back to work on Monday. And I didn't have a cast because I had this plate and these screws, and that holds everything together. You could actually see it in some shots, especially when I'm doing cooking in the kitchen. I wasn't able to really work the props as well, but I still tried to do it as much as possible. If you're looking for it, you can see that I'm favoring my right hand. And it was also kind of delicate, too, because there was no cast, so any little touch or any movement would kill. And then, of course, we had the Vegas episode where the big brawl happens and I run in and throw the punch. During a rehearsal, I went in and I threw the punch and during the melee, my arm got stuck in someone's arm, and it just kind of got twisted around again and that was a nightmare. That hurt.

You've become pretty good friends with the other guys on the show.
Yeah, we hang out all the time. We used to go to the clubs. I don't go out too often anymore, but still I will once in a while. Lately, I got Jerry into golf, so that's something we're doing a lot together now. I've been doing that with Mark, too. Mark and I play a lot of golf together. And now Jerry's got the bug.

You and Jerry play a lot of video games too.
I turned him onto "Guitar Hero." But I brought it over to his house and we were playing it and when I left, I said, "Go ahead, you play around with it for a while." And he got so into it, he exceeded where I was. If you get a couple of songs right, you get a new song. And he unlocked all these great songs for me—"Free Bird" and a bunch of others. It's a great game.

Jerry was actually the best man at your wedding, right?
It was kind of a last-minute thing. I found out that I had a Friday off and Monday off. I was like, "Wow, we've got four days. Babe, let's go to Vegas and get married." We had been engaged for about a year and a half, and at the time, we had a little one on the way, so we were eager to get married before the baby was born. I knew that I wasn't going to get too many chances because of this shooting schedule. So we decided on a whim to just go. I might've called Kevin Connolly first because I was thinking Kevin Connolly's got Vegas wired pretty well. He told me that he would be interested in going. I said, "I'm going to call Jerry right now." Jerry said, "Yeah, let's do it. This would be a trip." Unfortunately, Adrian and Jeremy were working. So we met in Vegas at the hotel and started working the phones. I had to run into downtown Vegas, which is a wild little place, and get the certificates. Then I had to run out and buy some rings and find a nice Elvis chapel. I'm a big Elvis fan. So we did it. Jerry Ferrara was my best man. He held the rings and Kevin Connolly walked my fiancée down the aisle and it was just really a good time.

Were you prepared for the success the show has had?
I had a gut feeling. The five main guys all work so well together. The way we bounce the dialogue together, it's got a fast pace to it. They put all the right characters together, and I think that that's half the battle with these shows. You've just got to find the right guys.

I don't know where I came up with that stuff. I was just thinking of *Zoolander* poses. You know, that face where you get the eyebrow down a little bit and you just pose. I wanted to have a cool face for the director to cut out of. You cut out of the pose and bang, you're out of the shot. Something funny. The other headshots they used were actually my old headshots. We thought it would be fun to see me with wild curly hair. And it was pretty funny, seeing those old shots.

JOHNNY CHASE

51

CAREER HIGHLIGHTS

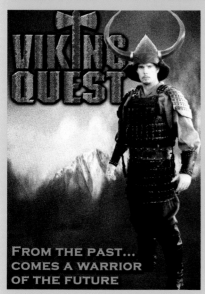

FROM THE PAST...
COMES A WARRIOR
OF THE FUTURE

VICTORY!

FROM DIRECTOR ED BURNS

FIVE TOWNS

THE WATCH:
Oakley Titanium Minute Machine. The shirt: Hugo Boss. The style: fashion-forward, sort of.

"Drama's style is the most L.A. because he's been living here the longest, but sometimes his look is a bit dated," explains costume designer Westcott about Drama's look. "He holds onto his past—his glory days. His style misses the mark a little bit, but he is trying. We try to find interesting clothes that are a little different.

"He's got a couple of themes I like to follow. We love bowling shirts—I get them vintage at stores in New York like Andy's Cheapies, and also from a company called Steady Clothing. He has a little bit of a Vince Vaughn thing going on—the tough working-guy that is working at being fashionable. The other company that I use for him

is J. Lindeberg, just to stick in a little trend here and there. We also dye a lot of shirts to keep them looking a little bit different that what's on the market. Other Drama themes include dragons, kung fu, snakes, skulls, and motorcycles. Drama wears a lot of jeans, and we use more

The Motorola I880 phone, perfect for fielding Lloyd's calls.

True Religion jeans and Frye boots are tough but still hip.

Paul Frank sunglasses for when Drama's feeling a little risky.

fashionable types like Rock & Republic, True Religion, AG Adriano Goldschmied, Kasil, and Juicy Couture.

"It's important to Drama that he gets the new things, as well as going to the places with the old stuff, so he would shop on Melrose and hit up the vintage shops for old bowling shirts, then swing over to Fred Segal/Ron Herman. They sell high-end contemporary clothing."

Steady bowling shirts say, "I loved *Swingers*, and this still works for me."

Nothing typifies Drama style like his Signature Drama Ray-Ban Aviators.

turtle ⤏

Jerry Ferrara

"I'm a total mama's boy," says Jerry Ferrara, who hails from Brooklyn's largely Italian, blue-collar neighborhood of Bensonhurst. It's no mystery why family comes first to Ferrara. His widowed mom (his father died when he was five) worked as a crossing guard near Ferrara's elementary school to provide a good life for her sons. "I saw her freezing on that corner so many times," Ferrara says. "Basically she did it so she would be off work when I got home." As a kid, Ferrara originally set his sights on becoming a professional basketball player. "Bensonhurst isn't the kind of place where acting is a common career path, and I've played sports all my life," he explains. "I was the tallest kid in my fourth-grade class. I've grown half an inch since then, so that kind of crushed my dreams." He later became interested in sports and broadcast journalism, but found his true calling while attending community college in Staten Island. Faced with unimpressive grades, he signed up for an acting class just to get an "easy A" and "That's where I caught the bug," he says. "The minute I walked in there, I said, 'This just feels like what I'm supposed to be doing.' And I've been doing it ever since."

First of all, what's Turtle's real name?
That's a great question. If you have any idea, I would appreciate if you told me because I have no idea. I know he will reveal it eventually, but it's going to be way down the road. Perrey, who plays Mrs. Ari, doesn't have a first name, either. I think a lot of the other characters have kind of been fleshed out and developed a little quicker than Turtle has, but there's a reason for that. He just moves through life slowly. Maybe that's why he's called Turtle. Who the heck knows? I'm starting to think maybe I may look like a turtle. But I can't get an explanation from the people who matter. They won't tell me.

Turtle's living large, but he's living off Vince. Is he as much of a parasite as he seems?

I think people misunderstand him. There are some people that would look at what he does, riding on his friend's coattails, and say, "Hell yeah, I would do the same thing." And there are other people that probably look at it and say, "He's lazy. He's a bum. You know, what does he do?" They've just got to realize with these four guys and even Ari now, they would do anything for each other, and if Turtle was a

Your first job in L.A. didn't have much to do with acting, did it?

My first job in Los Angeles actually was in a Boston Market. I didn't have a car out here my first two years, and everyone who lives in L.A. knows if you don't have a car, it's like a jail sentence because public transportation's not really that good. So I took a job at Boston Market because it was across the street from my apartment. I was responsible for all the chicken. Cooking it, cutting it up, serving it; I was the chicken man. I think I would

Entourage fashion, we took a private jet to Vegas. I had never been on a private jet before. And I hate flying, so it was an experience. And we had like ringside tickets to Roy Jones-Tarver, the first one. And I got to say, it was genius on Mark's part because no one knew each other before going into this. And that Vegas trip was definitely essential. We drank together. We gambled together. We went to clubs. We had a ton of laughs, and by the end of that trip we had that history that we needed to portray guys who know

57

famous actor or a famous musician or whatever and was filthy rich, it would be the same exact thing, just the roles would be reversed. All those guys would be living with him, and Vince would probably be managing his career. He'd do the exact same thing. I would say he's almost like the little brother of the crew or the mascot of the crew. Like, he's very easily bossed around. But I think that deep down, he wants to do something with his life. He doesn't want to live off of Vince forever...maybe for another ten years, but not for the rest of his life.

average like sixty-two hours a week and I would clear like 280 bucks. My first acting job didn't come until months after that. It was an episode of *King of Queens*.

You did an independent movie called *Cross Bronx*, which Stephen Levinson saw and subsequently asked you to audition for *Entourage*. After you were cast, Mark Wahlberg flew all of you to Las Vegas, right?

Yeah, it was two weeks after we got the job. We had all gone to dinner in New York once or twice, and Mark just put this trip together. In true

each other their whole life. We had that history the minute we came back.

What were your first impressions of the other guys?

My first impression of Kevin Dillon immediately was like, "Me and this guy will get along." Just judging by the way he holds himself, I knew we'd get along. He's a guy's guy. Kevin Connolly, I felt like I grew up with my whole life. The minute I sat down and talked with him, I'm like, "I feel like I've known this kid for

ten years." Adrian [Grenier], I met last. I'd never really met anybody like him. He's into rock and roll. He's in a band. There are some rock-and-roll songs I love, but I wouldn't go to a rock-and-roll concert. And he likes really obscure bands. He won't go see the Stones. He'll go see some weird band from Minnesota. So I didn't know how that was going to go at first, but looking back on it four or five years later, he's very much like me. Adrian and I have a lot of things in common.

Are you and Turtle alike in any ways?
I'm so not like that guy. I've been with my girlfriend for a while. I'm absolutely in love. I don't go out to clubs and chase a million girls. I was raised by my mom, and I wouldn't walk up to girls when I was single and say, "Hey, you want to go back to my house and fuck?" I would never in a million years, and I know I sound like a goody-two-shoes, but it's just the truth. I don't have that in me. The way I'm like him, I would say, is that I'm an extremely, extremely loyal person. My friends are my family. Like Turtle is with Vince and all those guys—he would do anything for them, as lazy and as stoned as he is, he really would do anything for them. I'm the same way with my friends. And their dialogue, that's how I talk to my friends. I break my friends' balls nonstop and they break mine nonstop.

What about the video games? Are you as much of a fan as Turtle?
Oh, huge. I'm into all the sports games like "Madden" and "NBA Live." I'm also into "Halo." I'll play anything, man. I really am like the ultimate gamer. I have the 360, PlayStation 3, PlayStation, even an old Xbox. I'll even go back to Atari. It takes up a lot of my time.

Your character is always wearing New York jerseys. In real life, who's your team?
The Knicks are my team. Every time I'm home, I go to all the games. I went back in their locker room and met all of them, and I've done a lot of interviews and stuff for MSG. MSG is a local channel in New York. I did a commercial for them that Spike Lee directed. It wasn't for a lot of money. I didn't even want money. I said, "If you can get me courtside tickets, I'll do ten commercials for you."

Do fans of the show want to smoke weed with you?
Everybody. The first thing they always say is like, "Yo, I got a blunt in the car, if you want to go smoke." I think it's kind of a blessing that I don't smoke anymore because if I did, I'd probably take a lot of those people up. And that's not really that good. You know, it's like a stranger giving you candy. Are you really going to smoke someone else's shit?

So what's actually in Turtle's bong?
They have this herbal tobacco, which most everybody uses, especially if you don't smoke cigarettes. But I've found that that stuff gives me a bad stomach ache and it will actually delay shooting because I usually have to run back to my trailer if I smoke that stuff. I smoke cigarettes, so I just smoke regular tobacco in the bong, American Spirit tobacco. It looks like weed smoke, but it's really harsh the tenth take. Everyone thinks it's real. It's like, "Come on, if I smoked that much weed while working, it would be the worst show in the world. Or at least my character would be the worst character in the world."

JERRY FERRARA ON BEING ATTACKED BY AHNOLD THE ROTTWEILER

The whole time we shot, I had food poisoning. I ate some bad chicken and had like a 102 fever. I was throwing up, and I was scared shitless. It's a Rottweiler, you know? I mean, they're sweet dogs, but they could do a lot of damage if they really wanted to. It turned out, most of the time, the dog was licking me. He wasn't even attacking, so I think that's why they shot it in a lot of wide angles. But they even had one point where he latches onto my crotch. They put a biteplate down there, and he ends up dragging me around the driveway. That never made it into the show, but it was scary the first few times. Once we got to take six or seven, I was all warmed up, and it was fun.

BEHOLD.

THE NIKE FUKIJAMAS

ONLY 200 PAIRS TOTAL IN EXISTENCE, and Turtle loses out to DJ AM at the last minute. Luckily, Vince is willing to drop $20,000 for some custom kicks from the famous graffiti artist. So how did the writers come up with this Season Three episode about Turtle's sneaker fetish? "Rob Weiss and Lev are crazy sneakerheads," explains Brian Burns, who wrote the episode. "I'm into sneakers, but nothing like these two guys. Over one hiatus, Rob Weiss was going down to these stores—Union and Undefeated—and buying his sneakers. He heard about all these kids waiting in line to buy limited editions. And we just thought, That's such a perfect Turtle thing."

A Sidekick for the world's best sidekick

60

Saigon's gift to Turtle, designed by Tim Schultz

FOR CASUAL
RITMO Rockstar

FOR DRESS
RITMO Impero

With all the hat-wearing, sunglasses aren't always required—but when they are, Oakley Whys are Turtle's pick.

Always Be Matching An Adidas New York Knicks jersey with matching pants and a New Era Knicks hat (left), and a Puma tracksuit with a Marc Ecko shirt and a New Era Yankees hat.

"With Turtle, it's a matter of matching everything to within an inch of its life," costume designer Westcott explains. "He's the most East Coast. There's a very big difference between what people can get away with here and what they can get away with there. Here on the West Coast, there is a lot more bling and accoutrement. Except for the custom necklace from Saigon, he doesn't wear chains.

"We have insane hats. We probably have about 400. I work with Kangol and New Era to get caps that match his sneakers and clothing.

"It seems like we have every color of Air Force Ones imaginable. I work with Nike directly, and they hook me up with whatever's new, and every sweatsuit and T-shirt has to be matched. and that's fun. We do a ton of

jerseys, too, but we keep it all New York teams—only Knicks and Yankees. We also work with different companies like Ecko, Sean John, and Zoo York. But his jeans are very straightforward. They're oversized, but the most we will do is a little design on the pocket, like Rocawear. And I would say as far as sneakers are concerned, he has like 125 pairs."

Episode Guide
Season 2 : Takeover

Episode 1: **The Boys Are Back In Town**

> **Airdate: June 5, 2005** | **Directed by Julian Farino** | **Written by Doug Ellin**

The boys return to L.A. after a summer shooting *Queens Boulevard* in New York ready for their next project. Ari pitches them *Aquaman*, but Eric and Vince have their sights set on the Pablo Escobar biopic *Medellin*. E reunites with his girlfriend, Kristen, but she's holding him off sexually. Drama, ready to dive headfirst into the acting game, goes off to update his *Outsiders*-era headshot.

Episode 2: **My Maserati Does 185**

> **Airdate: June 12, 2005** | **Directed by David Nutter** | **Written by Doug Ellin & Cliff Dorfman**

Ignoring Ari's pleas for them to give *Aquaman* a chance, the guys go to a beach party thrown by Jaime Pressly. Suspecting Kristen was two-timing him over the summer, Eric hooks up with a Perfect 10 model. When E's suspicions are confirmed, he breaks up with Kristen, but not before revealing his own extra-curricular activities. Drama thinks that calf implants are the key for landing a gig on the body-conscious show *Point Doom*. ➤ Ellin enjoyed shooting a scene at the Lakers game so much, he would return in Season 3, though, as he says, there was a difference: "The first year they were nice enough to let us do it when we were nobody. Then the second year when all the players knew the guys, they would come over and tell them how much they liked the show."

Episode 3: **Aquamansion**

▶ **Airdate: June 19, 2005** | **Directed by Julian Farino** | **Written by Rob Weiss**

Drama may have been a regular at the Playboy Mansion in his earlier heyday, but these days, he's persona non grata at Hefner's crib, after allegedly letting Hugh's monkeys out of their cages. While Drama figures out a way to clear his name, Vince looks into a mansion of his own—Marlon Brando's $4 million estate. The boys sneak Drama into the Playboy party, and Drama gets to set the record straight, laying the monkey cage catastrophe at the feet of Pauly Shore.

Drama →	What in the fuck are you saying?	
Ralph →	I told you. I didn't do it.	
Drama →	Just admit you did it.	
Ralph →	I, I told ya. I didn't. I didn't do it. I already told you that. You...ex-evening soap star.	
Drama →	I just did an indie, asshole.	

Episode 4: **An Offer Refused**

▶ **Airdate: June 26, 2005** | **Directed by Leslie Libman** | **Written by Doug Ellin & Chris Henchy**

$150,000 for an interior decorator? $50,000 for a fish tank? $10,000 for Drama's calf implants? With no payday in sight, E's concerned that the guys are descending into serious debt. Fortunately, good news arrives when the guys learn that *Queens Boulevard* earned a spot at Sundance. On the heels of the Sundance announcement, Ari tries to secure Vince the title role in *Aquaman*, but its director, James Cameron, has Leonardo DiCaprio in mind.

Episode 5: **Neighbors**

▶ **Airdate: July 3, 2005** | **Directed by Daniel Attias** | **Written by Doug Ellin & Chris Henchy**

The guys get the news—Leo is no longer in the running for *Aquaman*, paving the way for Vince to don the Aquasuit. All they gotta do now is convince James Cameron that Vince is the man for the role—and convince Billy Walsh to show Mr. Cameron *Queens Boulevard*. Calming tensions is Staci, the girl Vince has been seeing. The boys meet their new neighbor, Bob Saget, first when he brings over DVDs and pastries, then at Staci's house. Turns out Staci is also a Hollywood madam, which works out nicely for Turtle, who is in the midst of an epic dry spell.

Episode 6: **Chinatown**

▶ Airdate: July 10, 2005 | Directed by Julian Farino | Written by Larry Charles & Brian Burns

Looking for a quick payday to keep up his lifestyle, Vince takes a starring role in a commercial for the "Asian Red Bull." Aside from the cash, Vince gets to learn a few moves from the ad's hot stunt coordinator. Turtle, meanwhile, is a master fighter in his own right—in Xbox boxing. His secret? He can only play when stoned, a problem when the guys mess with Turtle and tell him there's drug testing at the tournament. Meanwhile, E tries to get James Cameron to screen *Queens Boulevard* at Sundance. ▶ Says writer Brian Burns, "We had an Xbox in the office and we were addicted to this boxing game, so one of us just said, 'We're going to have to find a way to make this constructive and not just us goofing off.'"

Episode 7: **The Sundance Kids**

▶ **Airdate: July 17, 2005** | **Directed by Julian Farino** | **Written by Rob Weiss & Stephen Levinson**

Vince and the guys touch down in Utah, planning to take Sundance by storm. *Queens Boulevard* is set to premiere, and Eric has convinced James Cameron to attend the screening. E, along with Ari, has also managed to get Vince an offer from Sundance king Harvey Weingard to star in the surfing saga *Tapping the Source*—the only problem is it shoots the same exact time as *Aquaman*. Meanwhile, Turtle and Drama duel for the affections of their gorgeous driver, Cassie. ▶ For safety reasons, producers wanted Grenier and company to take the chair lift down the mountain (after filming the episode's downhill snowboarding finale), but the foursome rebelled by snowboarding down instead. The direction for this episode was nominated for an Emmy

Episode 8: **Oh, Mandy**

▶ Airdate: July 24, 2005 | Directed by Daniel Attias | Written by Doug Ellin

Now that the guys have secured a sick crib for the summer—Jessica Alba's house in Malibu—and a sick new project, *Aquaman*, the focus shifts to finding a leading lady. While James Cameron has compiled an A list, his first choice, Mandy Moore, might cause a problem. Vince and Mandy used to be a serious couple, with a serious breakup. The prospect of seeing her again is enough to make Vince question whether he wants to continue working on the movie. Drama has a run-in with a surfer on the Pacific Coast Highway, which ends with the guy getting a nine-iron across the windshield of his PT Cruiser. ▶ Connolly got his friend, skater Chad Muska, cast in the part of Drama's road-rage victim. "They were like, 'Yo, we need a guy,'" Connolly recalls. "I was like, 'Yo, I got the guy.'" The episode was nominated for its direction.

67

Episode 9: **I Love You Too**

▶ Airdate: July 31, 2005 | Directed by Julian Farino | Written by Doug Ellin

The guys head to Comic-Con to announce that Vince will be starring in *Aquaman* with Mandy Moore. Vince risks the wrath of an influential Internet journalist, R.J. Spencer, when he walks off the interview, but E brings in the Pussy Patrol, a team of crime-fighting porn stars, to smooth things over. Drama, with plenty of geek-cred due to *Viking Quest*, finds himself sharing a dais with former costar Vanessa Angel. Back in L.A., Ari scores the entourage U2 tickets for Drama's birthday. ▶ The producers asked Bono to give a shout-out to Drama, but didn't know if or when he would do it. Bono surprised everybody by delivering the line, in Spanish.

Episode 10: **The Bat Mitzvah**

▶ **Airdate: August 7, 2005** | **Directed by Julian Farino** | **Written by Doug Ellin & Rob Weiss**

Ari invites the guys to his daughter Sarah's bat mitzvah. E overhears Vince tell Mandy that he still loves her on the *Aquaman* set. When E confronts Vince, Vince denies it and challenges E for the affections of Sloan, the beautiful daughter of Ari's boss, Terrance. Back from a long sabbatical, Terrance has made up his mind to steal Vince from Ari. Turtle and Drama, high as kites at the party, just want some freaking food.

Episode 11: **Blue Balls Lagoon**

▶ Airdate: August 14, 2005 | Directed by Daniel Attias | Written by Brian Burns

Drama gets the chance of a lifetime when he stars with his teenage crush, Brooke Shields, on a Movie of the Week. Now, if only Drama had better control over his, uh, emotions. Vince and Mandy find themselves on "Page Six" after a romantic weekend. When Ari learns that Terrance has set up a secret meeting between Vince and Quentin Tarantino, he tries to win Vince back by giving him a painting pulled right off his wall to give to Mandy. Too bad Eric figures out it's a fake. ▶ Shields is married in real life to Season 2 writer/producer Chris Henchy, who appears in the episode as the writer who Drama blithely dismisses as his competition for Brooke Shields's affections.

Episode 12: **Good Morning Saigon**

▶ Airdate: August 21, 2005 | Directed by Daniel Attias | Written by Stephen Levinson & Rob Weiss

Eric thinks that Vince's relationship with Mandy might be a problem when Vince oversleeps and misses his physical for *Aquaman*. Eric's not the only one who's worried, as Barbara Miller, Mandy's agent, teams up with Ari to grill E about the stars' relationship. Turtle finds a rap demo mistakenly left in E's car and tracks down the rapper, Saigon, after selling the song to Billy Walsh for the final credits of *Queens Boulevard*.

69

Episode 13: **Exodus**

▶ **Airdate: August 28, 2005** | **Directed by Julian Farino** | **Written by Doug Ellin**

Ever since Terrance came back into the fold, Ari's relationship with the agency has been tenuous. Finally it comes to a head when Ari stages a coup d'état, but his plan is thwarted when Adam Davies, a junior rival, reveals it to Terrance. Ari, without his company car, is chauffeured to his house by Lloyd, who delivers a most inspiring pep talk. Vince's relationship with Mandy looks like it's over, as Turtle and Drama spy her walking around Beverly Hills with her ex-fiancé. ▶ The episode, nominated for an Emmy for the writing, included Ari's code word for the secret meeting, "tsetse fly." The phrase was an homage to Ellin's favorite film, 1979's *The In-Laws*, in which star Peter Falk talks about the winged creatures.

Episode 14: **The Abyss**

▶ **Airdate: September 4, 2005** | **Directed by Julian Farino** | **Written by Doug Ellin & Rob Weiss**

Even three French maids can't stir Vince after his breakup with Mandy. He wants off *Aquaman*, which makes E question his business—and personal—relationship with Vince. Turtle sets up a showcase for Saigon, while E considers taking a job with Terrance. Ari struggles to round up his clients, but keeps Vince, who remains undecided about *Aquaman* until the last second. ▶ Connolly and Reeves had a running joke during the second season that they had never had a scene together, which is why Ellin wrote in a quick exchange at Ari's house. Says Reeves, "That was our big scene. We were like, 'Oh my God! We're finally getting to work together.'"

CHAPTER 3

hollywood
art, commerce, assistants, and adversaries >>>

VINCE'S CAREER HIGHLIGHTS

vincent chase

AN OTTO PARRISH FILM

HEAD ON

HEAD ON // This movie turned out to be Vince's big break, but the *Variety* review would have made less-secure actors move back in with Mom. "In *Head On*, a by-the-numbers crime thriller, only one thing is proven beyond a reasonable doubt; Vincent Chase is guilty of fraud. This fly-by-night pretty boy, who's been tapped as the 'It-Actor' of the moment, makes walking and talking seem so difficult that by the end, you wish someone would just let the man rest." Vince's reply upon hearing it? "At least he said I was pretty."

CHINESE ENERGY DRINK COMMERICAL → "I loved the idea of these famous actors who, here in the States, would just never put themselves in a regular beverage commercial," writer Brian Burns says. "Obviously over in Japan and even parts of Europe, they do this stuff all the time. You know, only an actor could go out and make half a million dollars tomorrow for a few hours work."

QUEENS BOULEVARD

"I remember we were in Doug's office, talking about the idea of Vince doing this movie," explains writer Rob Weiss. "The 'I am *Queens Boulevard*' line was just a throwback to that whole independent vibe of New York films. The guys are so clearly from Queens, so it just made more sense that they would go back and do their indie street film there. You know what I mean? Especially being guys who are from that neighborhood. So it was an obvious idea for us. I don't remember who actually spit it out, but whoever it was hit it pretty right on."

Starring **Vincent Chase**

Queens Boulevard

a film by **Billy Walsh**

EXECUTIVE PRODUCERS MARK WAHLBERG STEPHEN LEVINSON DOUG ELLIN LARRY CHARLES PRODUCERS MARK GREENBERG ROB WEISS JANACE TASHJIAN JULIAN FARINO CO-PRODUCERS BRIAN BURNS CASTING SHEILA JAFFE MEREDITH TUCKER DIRECTOR OF PHOTOGRAPHY STEVE FIERBERG COSTUME DESIGNER AMY WESTCOTT PRODUCTION DESIGNER STEPHEN McCABE WRITTEN & DIRECTED BY BILLY WALSH A BILLY WALSH ROBERT DUVALL PRODUCTION CO EXECUTIVE PRODUCER CHRIS HENCHY WRITING CONSULTANT CLIFF DORFMAN

AQUAMAN

"Working with James Cameron was unbelievable," Doug Ellin says. "With certain details, I get obsessed. When we started working on the episode, I was like, 'There's no other director. It's got to be James Cameron.' That was my feeling. One of our producers works with Cameron all the time. So I just wrote the script and she said, 'What the hell are you doing?' And I said, 'Come on, make a call.' And he said yes. And I never thought he would. There's nobody else who could have done it. Cameron was just like the greatest, most awesome guy. And then at the end of the season, he wrote me a letter about what could happen with *Aquaman*. He gave me five scenarios of what he thought could happen with the movie, which was just awesome. They were just so funny. He was like, 'Don't make the movie bomb.' And we had thought about making it bomb, but I'm like, 'It's James Cameron. It's going to be successful. Why wouldn't it be? The guy's never had a failure.' He was like, 'Don't make me look terrible.' He was totally joking, of course."

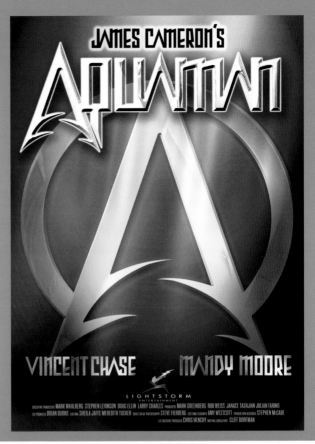

MEDELLIN

This gritty drama was to be Vince's *Scarface*, but instead it became both his biggest hope and heartbreak. He was supposed to make it with Paul Haggis until duplicitous dealmaking caused the film to fall apart. But Vince could never seem to get *Medellin* off his mind. In the Pablo Escobar story, the often-indecisive actor not only found his passion project, but his focus as an artist as well.

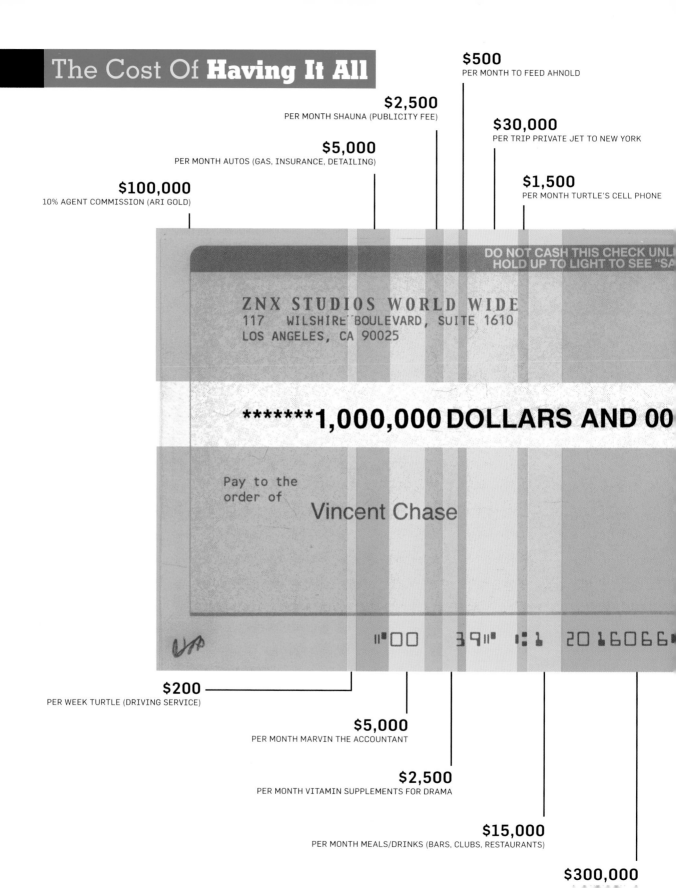

The Cost Of **Having It All**

$500
PER MONTH TO FEED AHNOLD

$2,500
PER MONTH SHAUNA (PUBLICITY FEE)

$30,000
PER TRIP PRIVATE JET TO NEW YORK

$5,000
PER MONTH AUTOS (GAS, INSURANCE, DETAILING)

$1,500
PER MONTH TURTLE'S CELL PHONE

$100,000
10% AGENT COMMISSION (ARI GOLD)

DO NOT CASH THIS CHECK UNLI
HOLD UP TO LIGHT TO SEE "SA

ZNX STUDIOS WORLD WIDE
117   WILSHIRE BOULEVARD, SUITE 1610
LOS ANGELES, CA 90025

*******1,000,000 DOLLARS AND 00

Pay to the
order of

Vincent Chase

⑈⑈OO   39⑈⑈ ⑆⑆ 2016066

$200
PER WEEK TURTLE (DRIVING SERVICE)

$5,000
PER MONTH MARVIN THE ACCOUNTANT

$2,500
PER MONTH VITAMIN SUPPLEMENTS FOR DRAMA

$15,000
PER MONTH MEALS/DRINKS (BARS, CLUBS, RESTAURANTS)

$300,000

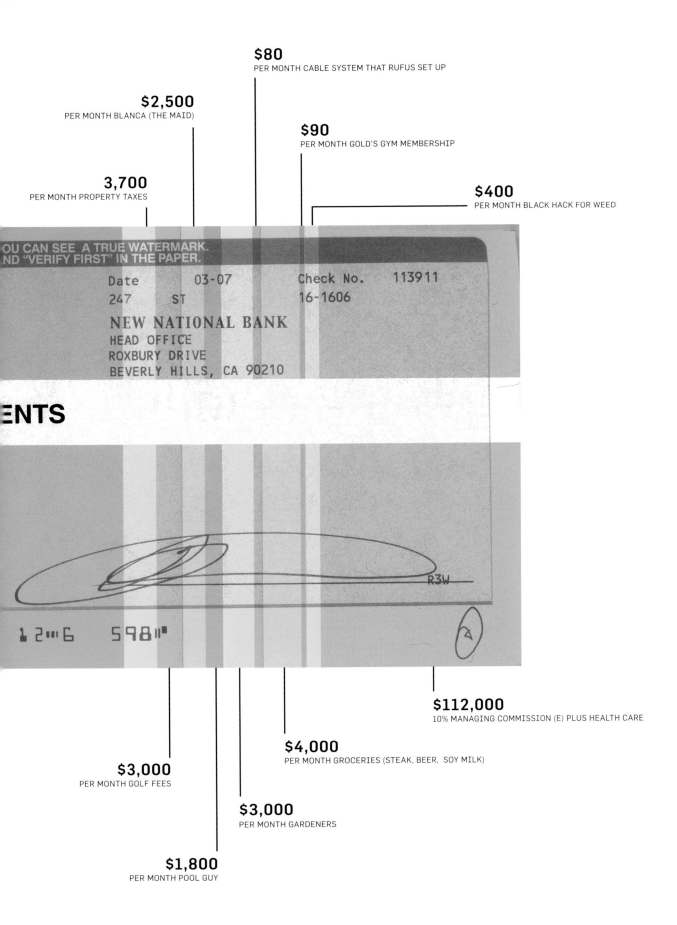

$80
PER MONTH CABLE SYSTEM THAT RUFUS SET UP

$2,500
PER MONTH BLANCA (THE MAID)

$90
PER MONTH GOLD'S GYM MEMBERSHIP

3,700
PER MONTH PROPERTY TAXES

$400
PER MONTH BLACK HACK FOR WEED

OU CAN SEE A TRUE WATERMARK.
ND "VERIFY FIRST" IN THE PAPER.

Date   03-07   Check No.   113911
247   ST   16-1606

NEW NATIONAL BANK
HEAD OFFICE
ROXBURY DRIVE
BEVERLY HILLS, CA 90210

ENTS

R3W

1 2 6   598

$112,000
10% MANAGING COMMISSION (E) PLUS HEALTH CARE

$4,000
PER MONTH GROCERIES (STEAK, BEER, SOY MILK)

$3,000
PER MONTH GOLF FEES

$3,000
PER MONTH GARDENERS

$1,800
PER MONTH POOL GUY

ari →

Jeremy Piven

Jeremy Piven's bravado-filled shark of a super-agent, Ari Gold, whose catchphrase, "Let's hug it out, bitch," has become part of the cultural zeitgeist, is probably best viewed as the physical embodiment of the entertainment industry itself: slick, smarmy, seductive, base, manipulative—but always compelling. And over the years, Ari has proven himself to be quite the paradox to both the actor who plays him and fans alike. Sure, he's an obscene, aphorism-spewing, assistant-abusing, cash-crazed power monger. But he's also a loving husband, a caring father, and a good friend to the guys. "I can't ever get ahead of this character," Piven says. "He's always dancing in some interesting dualities. But I know that I'm a very lucky man to be able to play this guy."

You went to your first meeting for *Entourage* in a "power suit."
Yeah, I just wanted to go in character. It's what actors do. We change our clothes in our cars—they're our traveling dressing room. So I changed in the car and went in there and we had a great conversation. I was probably thirty-five movies deep into my career at that point, but this is what you do. This is part of the journey. In this particular case with *Entourage*, I thought a meeting would've been really great and appropriate, and it was and it felt great.

Did you express any of your own ideas about playing Ari Gold at that meeting?
I bring my own ideas all the time. I love to contribute. I put it out there. From the get-go, I wanted to explore Ari's home life and his professional life. I think that they already had a very specific person in mind here. He's a family man who is also insanely driven. He's a beast, and so you have to be a beast. It's your job to step up. But I was interested in the duality of appearing to be incredibly crass and type A, and at the same time, loving my wife. Basically, I wanted to know where this guy came from, what his family is like and what makes someone want to have millions in the bank by the time he's forty or he's going to hurt someone. Because that's the way I thought of him. Now, we haven't yet explored all of these things with Ari, but listen, anything's possible. So I'm optimistic. You always got to stay optimistic, man.

Doug said that part of the reason HBO picked up the pilot was because of that scene in Koi. What do you remember about Ari's first face-off with E?
It was really fun. It's just so great to film in the town that you're portraying and go to these actual locations. I felt very equipped for that moment. There's no substitute for logging in the hours and that's what I did. So

it was really fun to get in there and mix it up. It went really well. What's interesting about the characters on this show is that they're all busting each other's balls. It's tough love everywhere.

How has Ari's relationship with Vince changed since the start of the show?
His loyalty and his love for Vinnie have always stayed the same. They've taken this journey and, at one point, they wanted to experiment with other people and places and it freaked them out. You know, it's hard when someone in a relationship isn't straight with you. I had an agent and he wasn't straight with me and, you know, I moved on. That's what happens. And in this particular case, it was Drama who promoted the philosophy of, "In the sea of sharks, you've got to go with a shark you know." And that was Ari. So they're back together again. They're back and I'm glad they're back. Ari has genuine love for Vince and has his back and would do anything for him and for his family.

We've been seeing Ari's life away from the office more and more lately.
I think we're starting to get into some more adult themes with him. I'm really happy with the way that it has progressed. I knew that it would produce great results, because sometimes it takes being exhausted and getting out of your own way to really hit something. Doug, in those later episodes, has made the writing so layered and interesting, like when my character has that breakdown. That's stuff that you kind of live for as an actor.

Ari does have some interesting dualities. He obviously loves Mrs. Ari, but earlier in the series, he made it seem like he was cheating on her.

I don't think he cheats on her. I think it's really interesting that the people who are the most garrulous are putting on the biggest veil, because they have the most going on inside. You know, like the lady doth protest too much? It's like, Ari stays monogamous, goes home to his wife, takes care of her in every single way, and then he's out, strutting around looking at every ass and showboating because that's his way. It's his outlet. He does that instead of actually pulling the trigger and cheating. And the more authentic I can make him look and seem and feel, the more interesting it'll be when it's revealed that he's not a cad. You're always playing within all these things, so it's pretty cool.

There's a lot of complexity with his relationship with Lloyd as well.
Ari and Lloyd are a match made in heaven because they're just so completely different. You have this foul-mouthed guy who will really stop at nothing and this incredibly sensitive gay Asian assistant. It's really just kind of genius. I love that relationship, and we're going to explore that more. Ari's revealed to have a soul, as you can see when he is incapable of selling Lloyd's ass out, which is really one of my favorite episodes.

But your Ari is largely a fictional character.
He is. And the great compliment is that I sometimes get people stopping me and saying, "Oh my God! I know who you're doing." And then they say, "It's Craig Jameson or whatever from some agency." They give me different names all the time. They all think Ari's behavior is based on someone they know, which means that we've landed on something that's authentic that they can relate to.

"Suits and more suits," costume designer Amy Westcott says about dressing Ari. "We have a few casual opportunities with him, but mostly, it's suits. And the thing is with him is that he's ahead of the game. He's trying to stay ahead of the rolling ball. There is a school of thought that people with a whole lot of power don't need to really get dressed—but not Ari. He's showing everybody that he's the best. Jeremy [Piven] wanted to avoid the obvious choices. That's been done and he's trying to stay ahead. The idea with him is power. He can get away with a purple shirt because

he's that good, you know what I mean? He's showing everybody that he started this company and he's at the top of his game. His wardrobe has to match his character or is going to look boring and typical.

"I use a lot of Dolce & Gabbana, Gucci, Ted Baker, Zegna, and John Varvatos. We use Gucci shoes for him. I have a lot of Prada shirts because they just fit him very well. He likes the earthy tones. He has an athletic build.

82

○ **THE POWER GADGETS:**
The BlackBerry Pearl
and the Motorola Krazer

He's wide in the shoulders and smaller at the waist. But his suits have to fit, that's the thing. I mean, a guy like him would shop on Rodeo Drive, and have everything altered to fit. He doesn't have a single tie that is under $150."

CLASSIC, EXPENSIVE, INTIMIDATING: The Oliver Peoples sunglasses

A killer agent doesn't need to dress like the rest: A Ted Baker suit, Brioni shirt, and Zegna tie (left) says, "I'm not boring." A Versace suit, Brooks Brothers shirt, and Gucci tie says, "I will win every time."

The Miller Gold Agency

Chase Harlan ➔ Art Director

When we were designing the office for the Miller Gold Agency, we decided to have the look of the actual agency where the real Ari Emanuel works. It's a famous building that made waves when it opened in the '90s, because it shocked the conservative-minded idea of what an agency should be. The building was hip, it was modern, it was youthful and bright and colorful. This was a huge contrast and a shocking kind of visual statement that reflected a new kind of voice for a hipper, younger, cooler agency that probably felt better to a lot of its clients than, say, an old-school agency that's marble and brass and mahogany wood.

We wanted to make it feel like life in a fishbowl. You can see through all of that glass, which gives the feeling that Ari's always watching: He's all-powerful, all-knowing, and would be watching his employees' every move all the time.

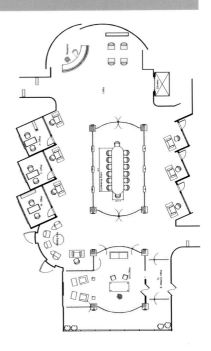

The plans created by Chase Harlan for the Miller Gold Agency offices.

NINE RULES
OF SUCCESSFUL AGENTING

It's usually Drama who breaks off the bitter chunks of hard-won Hollywood wisdom for the guys, but Ari also has his Yoda-like moments of enlightenment about doing daily battle in the dog-eat-dog world of the entertainment industry. Beyond his signature "Let's hug it out, bitch," Ari, who, if you recall, is a Harvard graduate with a JD/MBA from Michigan, has imparted several indispensable maxims for succeeding in showbiz. Future agents—we suggest pulling out your Monte Blancs and taking notes.

1 ALWAYS KEEP YOUR CONSCIENCE IN CHECK "No confessions," Ari says to Eric, who is contemplating telling his on-again/off-again girlfriend Kristen about his infidelity with the Perfect 10 model. "Did you read the paper, you idiot? Did you hear about this guy? He confessed to a murder in 1973 with no clues. Yeah, they're gonna give him twenty-five years. Shut your mouth. Do not say a word. Or you will just end up being gang banged by a bunch of cholos. Just relax. It's Hollywood, baby. Everyone strays sometimes." (Season 2, Ep. 2: "My Maserati Does 185")

2 HEALTHY BODY=HEALTHY MIND "It's pretty urgent that in the fifteen minutes a day I have free, I take time to keep this body fit," Ari tells Lloyd while doing some yoga-warrior poses on his office floor. "And not just so you have a great ass to look at. I want to live." (Season 3, Ep. 1: "Aquamom")

3 APPEARANCE IS MORE IMPORTANT THAN REALITY "Baby, it wasn't the Cubs' fault when that douche-bag grabbed the foul ball either, but they still don't get a World Series ring," Ari says to Mrs. Ari when rolling blackouts threaten to limit *Aquaman*'s opening weekend box office. "There are no asterisks in this life. Only score-boards. (Season 3, Ep. 3: "One Day in the Valley")

4 KEEP YOUR CLIENT REVIEW-PROOF "It does matter, alright?" Ari explains to Eric after Vince receives an unflattering review in *Variety*. "Everyone in town reads this thing. I got more calls about this stupid-ass thing than when my mother passed away. Alright? We got reviews coming out on Friday. Two hundred of them. If they're like this, we're in deep shit. That's why you book your next job before the movie comes out." (Season 1, Ep. 2: "The Review")

5 DESTROY ALL ENEMIES BEFORE THEY RISE TO POWER "That's why no more guys," Ari says to Eric after he learns that this former subordinate Josh Weinstein, now a Triad agent, is gunning for him. "You fire a guy, you create a rival. You fire a woman and you create a housewife." (Season 1, Ep. 6: "Busey and the Beach")

6 TREAT YOUR CLIENT LIKE A LOVER "Alright, here's what you do," Ari says to Eric about managing Vince. "You deal with talent the same way you deal with women. You have to make them believe that they need you more than you need them." (Season 1, Ep. 8: "New York")

7 ALWAYS MANAGE THE CLIENT'S EXPECTATIONS "Spider Man? Who said anything about Spider Man?" Ari barks at Eric after learning Vince's manager has set the star's sights on the webslinger's box office take. "Tell me that Vinny doesn't think we're gonna beat the biggest opening in movie history. Manage your client's expectations!" (Season 3, Ep .2: "One Day in the Valley")

8 UNHAPPINESS IS THE PRICE THAT WINNERS PAY "Of course he's not happy," Ari says to Eric after he learns that Vince is not exactly thrilled with how his career is progressing. "Nobody's happy in this town except for the losers. Look at me. I'm miserable. That's why I'm rich." (Season 2, Ep. 6: "Chinatown")

9 BAD NEWS IS NOT NEWS "First rule as an agent," Ari explains to Lloyd while avoiding Vince's calls after screwing up the Ramones project, "You never take an angry client's calls unless you have good news that will make him smile, alright? Now go make an excuse." (Season 3, Ep. 11: "What About Bob?")

By Ari Gold

Perrey Reeves

Meet the one person in Los Angeles who isn't impressed by Ari Gold's over-the-top antics: Mrs. Ari. Perfectly placid in her Chanel and Gucci, the statuesque more-than-a-trophy wife, played by actress Perrey Reeves, is kryptonite to Ari's super-bad behavior, bringing him to his knees with just a single, steely glance. Whether it's corralling him into couple's therapy or confiscating his cell phones at synagogue, Mrs. Ari is the glue that holds the Gold family together. "This big personality of Ari's—all bark, no bite—it doesn't really faze her," Reeves says of her character.

Your first day of shooting was a little stressful, wasn't it?
They had wanted to bring me in earlier for *Entourage*, but I wasn't available. And that's when Jeremy [Piven] said, "Just wait. Don't get someone else. She's so perfect for the role." That kind of support is so unusual in this business. So I had my last day of shooting on *Mr. and Mrs. Smith*, and that same night, I was scheduled for my first episode of *Entourage*. Fortunately, director Doug Lyman let me leave early. My first scene was where the Golds are coming out of the movie theater. HBO sent a car for me, and I went directly from our location on *Smith*, which was two hours out of town. We ended up going like 180 miles an hour to get there on time. I literally went straight into wardrobe. They showed me four tops, I picked one, put on some high heels, wore my own jeans, and they drove me

to the set with the same hair and makeup. The instant I arrived, they said, "Stand there and you're walking out of here." Then the cameras were rolling. Bam.

What's the one question that fans are always asking you?
Everyone wants to know what it's like on set working with this group of guys. I tell them I get to play a great, fun part with amazing people that I love. I get to work with Jeremy and I've got to tell you, there's really nothing much more fun than that. Our sets are pretty awesome because the minute the camera stops, Jeremy and I are usually laughing our heads off.

You knew Jeremy Piven previous to playing his wife, right?
My friendship with Jeremy Piven is just the six degrees thing. He and I have a lot of similar interests. He's

very interested in yoga, health, and wellness, so we have that in common. I heard that when they were considering people for this role and he saw that my name was on the list, he was like, "She's the one! Get her!" They had me do a little improv, you know, how would I do it? They weren't really sure the direction they wanted the part to go, and I just went in and kicked Ari's butt and there you go.

Does Mrs. Ari have an actual first name?
Doug said, "We'll call her Mrs. Ari, you know, just in our own heads." And then when I got together with Doug, I said, "You guys, you can never change that. That is hilarious. She doesn't need a first name." Because through the eyes of the *Entourage* guys, that's who I am. I am Mrs. Ari and as scary as Ari could ever be to them. You know

what I mean? I'm not afraid of him and they see the way she deals with him and they're like, "Oh, she doesn't take any of his crap," which is almost scarier than being a screamer.

Did you create a personal history for Mrs. Ari to better understand the character?
I had it in my head that she had gone to law school with Ari. I had all this great stuff. In my mind, Mrs. Ari gave it all up to have children, but she helped him do his deals. And then I came to find out from the writers that she was once an actress! I said, "Come on! That's not possible." But it turned out to be very funny because we've had some hilarious little moments. So Mrs. Ari has an artistic side. She became an actress to piss her parents off. I think she comes from a very conservative family in Connecticut. Ari's probably from Chicago. They're definitely not from California.

Ari can be such a self-centered bastard. So why does your character's marriage with him work?
They're in love. I mean, they're committed to each other. She is so behind him and you see that. Even though she gives him a hard time, she's helping to keep him from melting down. She's helping to take some of the pressure off of what he has to do all the time. In his professional world, he's always in charge. When he comes home and he knows the rules. There are boundaries that he must deal with because Mrs. Ari can't have him doing certain things. It's not healthy for the family life, which I think he's relieved by, secretly, underneath it all. It's like, thank God he doesn't have to go out and do that stuff—it's not like he's

89

in college any longer. But it's all good; it keeps everything cohesive and together. He's not wanting to get out of this marriage. This is his solid ground. He cares. He really does. And it's great.

How does Mrs. Ari feel about giving up her acting career to be a stay-at-home mom?
They don't have a nanny. Mrs. Ari is with those kids all day. They have three children, and she made the commitment to be the parent who raises them. But what are their names? We know Sarah's name. We did just find out that our son's name is Jonah (played by Doug Ellin's son, Lucas Ellin). And our other daughter—this is so embarrassing—but there was that episode when we went to her school. Mrs. Ari gets out of the car and goes over to get little whatever-her-name-is. Maybe her name is Shoshanna? I have no idea. So we did have a scene with her, but they never gave her a name.

Do you see any of yourself in your character?
The fact of the matter is that I'm playing a character. I mean, I'm

definitely a strong person, but I live in the jungle in Costa Rica when I'm not working in Los Angeles. My husband and I are building a yoga retreat center called Two Rivers, so it's sort of the antithesis of Mrs. Ari. We live on forty acres of beautiful property. It's all green, it's all solar and hydro—it's very opposite of L.A. I'm Miss Nature Girl. I've been a vegetarian my whole life. When people do realize it's me, they're like, "Oh my God. Oh my God. You're nothing like a Beverly Hills wife." Not that there's anything wrong with that, it's just different than I am.

What do people say about your character?
I have men come up to me all the time and say, "You remind me of my ex-wife," which is horrible, but I'll respond, "Oh, OK, well, I hope she was really hot." I think they're giving me a compliment, but they don't know how bad it sounds. I also have women who say, "If only I could have a little more Mrs. Ari in me and in my marriage." I don't know if that's a good thing or a bad thing, but hey, thanks for watching!

● ● ● ● ● ● ● ● ● ● ●

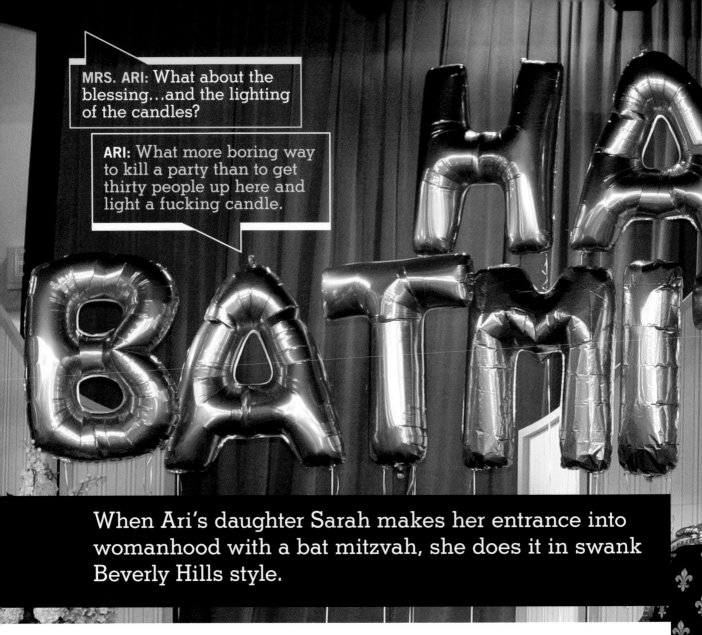

MRS. ARI: What about the blessing...and the lighting of the candles?

ARI: What more boring way to kill a party than to get thirty people up here and light a fucking candle.

When Ari's daughter Sarah makes her entrance into womanhood with a bat mitzvah, she does it in swank Beverly Hills style.

An A-list DJ is on the ones and twos, large sums of cash are rolling in (big boss-man Terrance drops $50,000 on the little lady), and mega-star and supercrush Vince Chase is in the house. Never mind the fact that his glassy-eyed friends are out in the kiddie area stuffing hot dogs in their faces, or that her father is his usual embarrassing, win-at-any-cost self. This is her party, and she's got the tiara to prove it.

Couple's therapy
is supposed to bring you closer,
right?

Not if you're Mr. and Mrs. Gold. For Ari and Mrs. Ari, time in the therapist's office is a minefield of marital mishaps and questionable communications skills. It doesn't help that Ari is always checking his BlackBerry, answering his phone, or blowing up in the face of his wife's perpetual calm. But while Ari might claim that marriage counseling is hurting his happiness, judging from his diminishing tantrums, the Golds' five therapists have calmed down his mercurial moods.

Ari's therapy thermometer

SESSION 1

Mrs. Ari wants to discuss Ari's anger management issues, but she's cut off when one of his cell phones rings—but not just any phone, it's Eric calling on the "Bat Phone" to let him know James Cameron is directing *Aquaman*.

BEST EXCHANGE

Mrs. Ari: I ask for one hour out of a day for his undivided attention and I can't even have that.

Ari: You can have it if you want to live in Agoura-fucking-Hills. And go to group therapy, but if you want a Beverly Hills mansion and you want a country club membership and you want nine weeks a year at a Tuscan villa, then I'm gonna need to take a call when it comes in at noon on a motherfuckin' Wednesday.

TEMPERATURE RATING

Break-the-glass ballastic

SESSION 2

Sex is the topic of today's meeting, and Ari is in an almost playful mood since it's *Aquaman*'s opening day and he's got reason to believe it's going to be a hit. But—surprise, surprise—that private line starts ringing again, and Ari's just got to take the call. This time it's Vince. Session over.

BEST EXCHANGE

Dr. Marcus: So when was the last time you had sex?

Ari: With each other, or...?

Mrs. Ari: Well, if you're not gonna take this seriously, Ari—

Ari: H-honey, I'm taking it seriously. It's just for the amount of money we're spending here, I could get you a pro to service even your most bizarre fetishes.

TEMPERATURE RATING

Seething yet playful

SESSION 3

Vinnie is gone and not even Mrs. Ari can fill the void. She's worried about the depression he's sunk into—he slept past 5:30!—but Ari isn't ready to admit to his separation anxiety from his favorite client.

BEST EXCHANGE

Ari: I have work to do. I have hundreds of clients to deal with. And just so we're clear, I don't care about any of 'em. Like wife number one and therapist number seven. Good day!

Mrs. Ari: You're really only our fifth.

TEMPERATURE RATING

Curiously calm

lloyd →

Rex Lee

Behind every great agent in Hollywood cowers an even greater assistant. When Lloyd took over the desk from Emily in Season Two, many wondered if his skin was thick enough to endure Ari's constant tongue-lashings. Of course, we quickly discovered that, in addition to his unwavering loyalty, Lloyd has the patience of Buddha and the ability to perform a special kind of

mental judo, taking Ari's insults and somehow turning them into terms of affection. And now the two are inseparable; he's become the much-needed yin to Ari's jabbing yang. "I'm playing Lloyd as if he saw the good in Ari much earlier than most," says Lee, who actually has first-hand knowledge of what it's

When did you first realize that you wanted to be an actor?
I'd say that as early as three, I knew I wanted to be an actor. But nobody really took me seriously. And I was easily dissuaded. The truth is, I didn't take my first acting class until I was in college. I went to Oberlin because they have a great music school, and at the time I thought I wanted to be a musician, a pianist. A complete mistake. That's not what I wanted to do with my life. So I took my first acting class and I thought, Wow, this is it. This is what I was meant to do. It took me a year or two before I decided that I was going to try to make a living as an actor. Well, once I did that, I felt like I was committed to this path. I've certainly had a lot of nonacting jobs to pay the bills, but I never wavered from my desire to make it as an actor. Before moving back to L.A., I worked as an assistant to various casting directors in commercials. I was pursuing acting, and I thought that if I worked in casting that it might

really like to toil as someone's assistant in Hollywood. (Before he became a regular on the show, he worked for several casting directors.) "I've had bosses in the past that were so concerned about their job that they forgot about the people around them," he explains. "So I guess I naturally have the impulse to give people the benefit of the doubt. Sometimes people behave badly, but it doesn't make them intrinsically bad." Well said, Lloyd.

help me get some auditions. And it did. I used to tell people that if God came down and said, "You're just not going to be an actor, don't even bother trying," I probably would've gone into casting, but luckily, that didn't happen. I learned a bit about acting working in casting. My very first day, I happened to be working for a guy who was auditioning Asian men and women about my age. He said, "Go ahead and audition." So I did, and the camera guy showed me the audition after I was done. The audition happened to be filmed in extreme close-up and I was mugging for all I was worth. I was making faces. I thought I was a subtle actor. It was the exact opposite of subtlety, and that was a great lesson to learn. As an actor, my perception of what I thought I was doing was just completely wrong. And now I'm on this show where if you're going for the big laugh, it's usually not as funny. More often than not, we're just trying to play the reality of the situation.

What were your first thoughts on the character of Lloyd? He wasn't always written as an Asian male, correct?
When I went in for an audition and got the sides, the role was clearly written for an African American. A month or two later, a reporter was on the set and we were talking and I told her about it and Doug Ellin overheard us and said, "Actually, we saw everyone in town for that role." They'd seen African Americans. They'd seen some women and a whole bunch of other people before they found me. Which is even more flattering in the long run. It's not like they immediately thought, We need an Asian guy.

Lloyd is obviously a smart and driven guy. Why does he let Ari talk to him like that?
My secret for playing Lloyd is a strange sort of reference. The first time Madonna was on *American Bandstand*, back in like '84, Dick Clark was like, "So what do you want to do now? What's next for you?" And Madonna looks straight into the camera and she says, "I'm going to rule the world." Lloyd's secret is that he wants to be as powerful as Ari. He wants the student to surpass the master. A lot of people ask me, "Why does Lloyd stay loyal to Ari? Why does he stay in that situation?" And I say, "Lloyd's very patient," which he is, and I sort of downplay how ambitious he is. But Lloyd is incredibly ambitious. I took my cue from the speech when Ari is leaving the agency, where I say, "I know the endgame, and you, Ari Gold, are it." I loved that line. It just triggered something in me.

Were you shocked when you first saw Lloyd's car? It seems like he would drive something far less flashy.
The first time I saw that car, I said, "Wow, that's a cool car. Whose car is that?" And they said, "Yours." And I literally had to stop and look at the car and wrap my mind around the idea, and then I said, "Oh, that's funny." It was sort of a non sequitur to me, and I guess that was part of the point. I think that's one of those details that people probably didn't even think about. I didn't think about what kind of car Lloyd drove until they presented me with this car. And it surprised the hell out of everybody.

Do you worry about the slurs hurled at your character?
I worry any time any character on any show or in any film says something that is prejudiced in some way. Having said that, I think of myself as an actor and an artist, and I totally understand that in the context of this piece, that kind of dialogue makes sense. I never go to Doug in a huff and say, "Why did he have to say that?" I trust that when the people who watch the show hear Ari say something homophobic, they realize it's homophobic. I want the relationship between Ari and Lloyd to be as real and as layered as possible. The fact that Ari says racist or homophobic things to Lloyd is part of the story of the two of them.

Is there really a gay assistant corps?
I'm not exactly sure if there's really a gay assistant mafia. When I was working in casting, there were a lot of gay assistants. But I don't think they were organized enough to have a name.

What's it like to work with Jeremy Piven?
Jeremy's a very skilled, talented actor. I don't think I truly understood until I worked on this show how great it is for an actor to work with other really good actors. Working with Jeremy has been really eye-opening, exhilarating, exciting, and informative. I think the biggest lesson I've learned as an actor is I have no choice but to be in the moment. And I don't think I ever realized how little I was in the moment until I started working with Jeremy. He likes to improvise, and you never know what's going to happen. I have to be the best that I can be to keep up with him. Every take is different. Not always wildly, maybe just subtly different, and I have to be aware of that if I'm going to do my job.

Are you recognized on the street by fans?
When I go out of my apartment, almost every day at least one person recognizes me and says something.

I get approached by real assistants all the time. It's funny because they always tell me where they work. They'll be like, "I'm an assistant at William Morris. I'm an assistant at Gersh." And then they'll tell me how much they appreciate how accurately I portray what happens when you're an assistant. The vast majority of them say, "My family in Illinois had no idea what I did until I told them to watch Lloyd on *Entourage*. That's me. That's my life!" As an actor, that's the best thing to hear.

We rarely see Lloyd outside of the office. What's he do in his spare time?
When he's not in the office, I think that Lloyd has a very active social life. Being the assistant to Ari Gold has given him a sense that he's someone in the world, so I think that he goes out into his own world and has a lot of friends and has a lot of confidence in social situations. I once had this idea: What if Ari had to go to Lloyd's apartment to sign a paper or something? I really thought it would be cute if Lloyd had three friends and he was like the Vince in his own entourage.

Anonymous Horror Story // Confessions of a Former Assistant

"The show is completely realistic," says a former assistant who worked for several top Hollywood agents. "Typically, your day involves anything from answering the phones, to taking notes, to sending out packages and letters, to reading scripts. And when you work for higher-profile agents, there's usually a huge personal component that comes along with working on the desk. Anything from making them breakfast at work, to servicing their pool and walking their dog. I worked for one agent who wouldn't even take his car to the valet himself. He would call me and I would come down and stand in the parking garage like an idiot and he would hand me his stuff. I'd get in his car and drive it down for him. But there are some perks to being an assistant. Believe it or not, you get girls. It's true. Girls will sleep with you because they think you can help them. It's all very Turtle-esque. If you're at a party and you're working for a good agent, other young assistants will find you more attractive."

"This is my theory behind Lloyd: His job is corporate, but his personality isn't. We keep him in conservative suits, very straightforward suits," costume designer Amy Westcott says about Lloyd's style. "But then he can have fun underneath. We have him in bold stripes, contrasting ties, colorful vests, and sweaters. That way, he's not going to look like everybody else in the office. He's color-coordinated and he's more bold than the rest of the people in the office. His suits are Brooks Brothers, but the underpinnings are from anywhere from Ted Baker to Diesel. He would shop at a good department store, like Saks or Nordstrom, or Neiman Marcus. But he is an assistant, so we have to keep things at a relatively realistic price point. Maybe he spends all of his earned money on clothing?"

The Palm Treo ► is the necessary evil that's essential for every agent's assistant.

100

The suits say business, but the shirts and ties say pleasure. From left: Brooks Brothers shirt and tie, Thomas Pink shirt and Ted Baker tie, and Thomas Pink shirt and BCBG tie.

The sunglasses make a statement:
I've seen the endgame.

Always, always
get to work be-
fore the boss: The
RITMO Centurion

Keep your head
down and your
hands free with
the Bang &
Olufsen earpiece.

LOVE MEANS NEVER HAVING TO SAY YOU'RE SORRY.

ARI (TO THE GUYS):
You like Gaysian Lloyd? He's cute, right? And he covers two quotas.

ARI: HEY LLOYD. GET THE FUCK IN HERE. I WANT TO MAKE OUT WITH YOU.

LLOYD: How did it go?

ARI: How the fuck did the Bay of Pigs go, Lloyd?

Ari (to Lloyd): CHOP CHOP!

Ari (to E, who hasn't been laid in months): Want me to get Lloyd in here and have him hari-kari you with his pecker?

ARI (SHOUTING DRUNKENLY OUT OF LLOYD'S CAR WINDOW): My life is over!

LLOYD: You'll bounce back, Ari Gold.

LLOYD: Can I vie for the ten grand prize?

ARI: Sure, but you'll get paid in yen.

ARI: Speak or I will intern you like it's 1942.

ARI: I drove to work in an $80,000 Mercedes and now I'm going home in a prop car from *The Fast and the Furious*. I just don't see it, Lloyd.

ARI: I WANT EVERY DESK TO BE STERILE ENOUGH FOR YOU TO GET TRAINED ON.

ARI: Why the fuck did you tell him I have a more important lunch? Do you think that's going to put a smile on his face?

LLOYD: What did you want me to say?

ARI: That I have a huge wart on my cock that needs removal would have been better. What the fuck, Lloyd?

ARI: Lloyd, what the fuck is this? **LLOYD:** It's your finger. **ARI:** It's dust Lloyd. It's fucking dust. Why is it here? **LLOYD:** The cleaning staff is on strike. You know that. **ARI:** They strike, you work. You're Asian. You're supposed to be a neat freak. Now go get a rag.

ARI:
Listen to me, Lloyd, do you want to make it or do you want to fold shirts at a Chinese laundry? Now pledge. Nod if you understand what I'm saying.

LLOYD:
I understand.

ARI:
You can't just fucking nod?

Ari:
Lloyd, pack up all my files. Pile everything you see into a box. Everything. You see a used condom, an executioner's mask, and a goddamn spiked paddle, don't think, just pack that bitch. Chop suey!

LLOYD (TO ARI):
Look. You said the first rule of an agent is not to call until you have good news. Well, you have no good news. But I have news for you, Ari Gold. Yes, you screwed up. Yes, you were devious. Yes, you were conniving. But yes, you care. I know that even when you throw the most hurtful, homophobic slurs my way that you really do care. Vince knows that. Just remind him.

Ari: He's coming. I'm actually nervous

Lloyd: That's cute, Ari.

Ari: Get out of my office Lloyd.

LLOYD:
You know I don't like to lie, Ari.

ARI:
Be a man, or as much as a man as you can possibly be, for God fucking sakes.

ARI: How is it to take it up the ass anyway, Lloyd?
LLOYD: I don't know, Ari. I'm a top.
ARI: Come on, really?

LLOYD:
I worked eighteen hours a day to save up the money to put myself through Stanford Business School. While I was there, I cleaned the cafeteria during the hours I wasn't studying and still graduated top of my class, only to take a job delivering mail to unappreciative overpaid little cock suckers. Then to finally get the big break that would allow me to answer your phones and be both racially and sexually harassed for the next nine months. But I know the endgame, and you, Ari Gold, are it. So stop with your fucking whining and go into your gorgeous three-million-dollar house with your beautiful goddess wife and figure out how you're going to make both our lives happen tomorrow.

ARI:
That was a good speech, Lloyd. Yeah. If I was twenty-five and liked cock, we could be something.

ARI:

LLOYD!

Lloyd: Are you happy, Ari? Or is this madness that will turn on a moment's notice?
Ari: This is happiness, Lloyd. This is pure heterosexual male happiness.

shauna →

Debi Mazar

Debi Mazar, who plays Vince's ultra-aggressive, yet still strangely nurturing publicist, Shauna Roberts, is a perfect fit for a show about New Yorkers trying their hand at Hollywood. Mazar grew up in Queens and Brooklyn before making her big-screen debut in director Martin Scorsese's *Goodfellas*. Adding to her credentials, she even hung out with Mark Wahlberg before he became a marquee name. "He was a fan of mine because he was a huge Scorsese fan," she says with a laugh. With a career that spans nearly two decades, Mazar was once connected with another famous entourage— that of pop singer Madonna. But she denies ever really being part of Madge's crew. "We're old friends and I've certainly gone out with her or met her at a party, but I've never been in her entourage and I've never had an entourage myself," Mazar explains. "I like to be able to talk to who I want to talk to and I don't like to babysit people. I can't move fast with an entourage."

You've been around basically since the beginning. What do you remember about the audition process? When I first went in for the show, the character of Shauna, the publicist, didn't exist. I went in to play a lawyer who was going to be a series regular. For Shauna, I created a backstory for her that was more or less just for me. She came out of New York, got to Los Angeles, and found a high-powered job in publicity. She barely has any personal life because publicists tend to work 24/7. Shauna takes care of any kind of press that Vince has to do for a movie or for his career.

She tries to make sure that if he gets in trouble, she squashes any kind of press leaks that there might be on little scandals, a girl he's dating, or if he's passed out in the club or wrecked a car. She also tries to put him at the right parties to meet the right people. She makes sure that the reporters get all the facts right when they write a story about him. At a premiere, she takes care of the car and gets him set up to walk the red carpet. She also makes sure that he's going to the premiere with the right woman. Hence, the episode when he took his mother.

How is *Entourage* different from other shows you've worked on?

The show has put me on the map as a woman with a strong voice, more than any other TV series that I've ever been on, and I've been on a few. I go to a mall like the Grove here in California, and people are like, "Hey, I like the show!" And I'm like, "You watch that?" I feel like they've made me a rock star.

DEBI MAZAR ON CHRISTY
the assistant publicist, played by Kate Albrecht

"She's great. It's so funny because when she first got the character, I took her under my wing because I loved the idea that I had my own personal assistant and we talked a lot about acting and stuff. I had no idea she was Chris Albrecht's daughter. And then one day, Chris came up to me at a function and he said, 'Thank you so much for being so kind to my daughter.' And I was like, 'Oh, you're welcome,' and then I was like, 'Who's Chris's daughter?' I just never put two and two together. Personally, I just always treated her like, you know, an actor for hire. She's a fantastic actress and it's been so much fun."

Debi Mazar collaborates with us one hundred percent. If she has a fabulous dress, she'll bring it in or we'll go shopping for the perfect ensemble. Basically she knows what I like and I have a good sense of what she likes, so we put our heads together. It is great to have her. She is so striking, and she has such a style about her personally, that she brings a lot to the character. Her style rides the line of masculine and feminine. It's a masculine look, but keeping the feminine details. So where we'd do a great Dolce & Gabbana white suit on her, we'd pair it with a sexy camisole and some amazing heels.

108

SHAUNA'S FINEST (AND DARKEST) HOURS AS VINCE'S PUBLICIST

The highs include prominent features in *Daily Variety* and the *Hollywood Reporter.* The lows: Her client's indiscreet romance as featured in "Page Six" and a *National Enquirer* feature about the Vegas fallout. Eric, control your client!

ENTERTAINMENT'S 1st DAILY PAPER

THE Hollywood REPORTER

a VNU publication

www.hollywoodreporter.com $2.99

VINCE CHASE SPECIAL ISSUE

Happy Birthday Vince

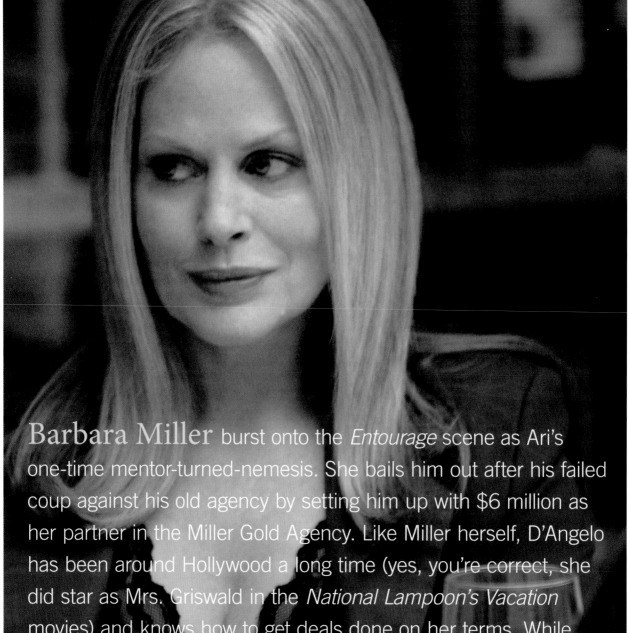

Barbara Miller burst onto the *Entourage* scene as Ari's one-time mentor-turned-nemesis. She bails him out after his failed coup against his old agency by setting him up with $6 million as her partner in the Miller Gold Agency. Like Miller herself, D'Angelo has been around Hollywood a long time (yes, you're correct, she did star as Mrs. Griswald in the *National Lampoon's Vacation* movies) and knows how to get deals done on her terms. While the actress doesn't shy away from giving her character sex appeal, she thinks Babs is way beyond needing it. "The thing about Barbara is that she is able to get what she wants directly. That's what I'm trying to say with her sexuality. She doesn't have to seduce somebody to get them to listen to her point of view."

How did you become involved with the show?

At the end of Season 2, I went in and talked to Doug because I was a huge fan of the series. He had an idea in mind and he wanted to bring on a character that was based on a couple of female agents— and one of them had been mine. Then we talked for a little bit about entourages in general. Being in Hollywood, I've seen a lot of entourages in my time. So at the end of the meeting, I said, "Well, look, I'm a big fan, so whatever you're doing with this role, keep me in mind. I mean, I'll do anything you want, you know?" And he said, "Go talk to Sheila." Sheila Jaffe's the casting director. And I said, "OK, thanks." So I went to Sheila thinking, I'll just make sure she has all my information. She said, "Here's the start date." I didn't even realize I had the part.

What do you remember about that first scene in the conference room with Ari and Eric?

When we shot my first scene, in the conference room, there was this one little improvised line that I threw in. We turned the camera around and it was on Kevin, and Jeremy said to me, "You've got the biggest cock in the room, Babs." And then I threw in this line, "Well, we haven't seen Eric's yet." Everybody cracked up. I improvised that line. After that was over, Doug said, "Well, would you guys like to form an agency?" And I said, "Whoa, wow, wow." That was at the end of Season Two and so I just crossed my fingers that I'd get a call. Then when they were gearing up for Season Three, I did get a call.

What is the key to understanding Barbara, a woman who has had so much success in a male-dominated business?

She's voracious, but Barbara is not inappropriate. Barbara does not do inappropriate things. She's not going to do blow in the bathroom, and she's not going to hit on Ari. But I will tell you one thing that Doug said—she doesn't lose control. That was really important to him. Let me put it this way: I'd say that her raison d'être is not to lose control. Obviously, this is a very strong character and a powerful character, and yet, in the workplace, quite powerful women are often portrayed as having a great deal of anger. Barbara Miller doesn't see herself as a bitch because she doesn't see herself as angry. I mean, she's just who she is and the power that she has is because she's been able to make the right decisions for a very long time.

Her cleavage is not gender neutral.

That's definitely something I brought to the role. Those weren't improvised in any way. They are completely natural.

How do you view agents?

Agents are basically destined to be middle men. They aren't producers, they aren't talent, so they're the jugglers. They're the people who have to figure out how to get everybody else in play. As far as weapons in their arsenal, they actually do have to come up with inventive ways of getting many, many people to agree to many, many things. What you hope for in an agent is somebody like Ari, who, at the end of the day, does have an emotional investment in his client.

What, in your opinion, makes this show so unique?

What's happening on that set is so alive. It's not like it's a series where everybody's just in their roles and they come there and say their lines and then they go home. It's not that kind of thing. I mean, this is alive. This is an actor's show. This is a writer's show. The actors go there to act. And they're really working. Everybody shows up and they're really, really, really working. And the cinematography is amazing, the direction is amazing. The amount of respect that is given for the acting that's done on stage is unbelievable. I know this sounds obtuse, but it's like trying to describe the ocean on any given day.

Why has this show been so successful connecting with audiences?

I think the reason that it's tapped into people's psyches outside of the business is because they recognize themselves in the characters. There's that joke of, "Are you a Vince? Are you an Eric? Are you a Turtle? Are you a Drama?" There's something in everybody that identifies with each person in this show according to where they are in their own lives. Are they in charge of their lives? Are they striving to be somebody? Are they falling short of their goals? Are they hanging onto somebody who's got more than they have? Are they putting their work before their family life? Are they a woman who's driven in the workplace? Do they have issues in the workplace with their employer? You know, like Lloyd. Doug's got an ability to write something metaphorically for everyone.

Episode Guide
Season 3: Supremacy

Episode 1: **Aquamom**

▶ **Airdate: June 11, 2006** | **Directed by Julian Farino** | **Written by Doug Ellin**

After Ari tells Vince he has to find a "premiere-worthy" date for the *Aquaman* premiere, Vince decides there's only one woman he wants to bring—his mother (played by Mercedes Ruehl, below). The problem is she hasn't been on a plane in thirty years. Turtle and Drama dodge an irate James Woods after stealing his tickets to the premiere. Ari, now the head of a small boutique agency, takes a $100,000 loan from his wife when his checks start bouncing. ▶ James Cameron took home one of the two aluminum triton spears made for the film's premiere to put in his production office.

Episode 2: **One Day in the Valley**

▶ Airdate: June 18, 2006 | Directed by Julian Farino | Written by Marc Abrams & Michael Benson

Turtle predicts a box-office opening for *Aquaman*: $114,844,117? ("One dollar more than Spider-Man made.") To check the reaction of the public, the guys head to a theater in the Valley, or "Hell's waiting room," as Drama calls it. When a full-scale California blackout hits, Ari stresses the possible negative impact on the opening weekend for *Aquaman*. Vince, never one to worry, makes a couple of geeks "almost famous" when he accompanies them to a high school party. ▶ The morning after the episode aired, a two-page ad ran in *Variety* touting *Aquaman*'s record-breaking "$116,844,114" box-office splash.

Episode 3: **Dominated**

▶ Airdate: June 25, 2006 | Directed by Julian Farino | Written by Rob Weiss

With a number-one movie at the box office and the *Aquaman* ride opening at Six Flags, life couldn't be much better for Vince and the crew. Then Dom, their buddy from the old neighborhood, comes back into their lives. Fresh from a stint in jail, Dom has come back to shop his handwritten script and drive the gang miserable by stealing Turtle's chauffeur duties and calling Eric "E-Bola." Meanwhile, Ari has to deal with child star—and first-rate wiseass—Max Ballard making moves on his daughter, Sarah. ▶ Domenick Lombardozzi was originally in the running to be a cast member of *Entourage*, but as Mark Wahlberg says, "We wanted Dom in the show, but he wasn't available. He was working on *The Wire*."

Episode 4: **Guys and Doll**

▶ Airdate: July 2, 2006 | Directed by Craig Zisk | Written by Rob Weiss & Doug Ellin

Aquaman has catapulted Vince to superstardom, and Ari and E are in agreement on Vince's next project: the Colombian drug drama *Medellin*. Vince and the guys head out to charm *Medellin* producer Phil Rubenstein at a launch party for Rubenstein's latest wine. Much to the group's surprise, it's Dom who comes through in the clutch and helps win over the producer. The role is put into jeopardy when Phil's beloved Shrek doll disappears, and the ex-con Dom is the obvious suspect. ▶ The late Bruno Kirby played Rubenstein, joining Chris Penn and Stanley DeSantis, who played producer Scott Wick, as actors who made one of their final onscreen appearances on the show.

Episode 5: **Crash and Burn**

▶ Airdate: July 9, 2006 | Directed by Patty Jenkins | Written by Brian Burns

With *Medellin* and *Aquaman 2* set to start shooting on the same day, Vince and E try to figure out a way to make both. E and Vince convince Warner Bros. chief Alan Grey to push back *A2*'s start date sixty-five days, twenty-five less than *Medellin* director Paul Haggis needs. While E works out a short shoot schedule with Haggis, Turtle works Ari to represent his suddenly hot rapper, Saigon. In between calls about Saigon from record labels, Ari rids his family of child star Max Ballard by convincing Penny Marshall to cast the kid in a film set in Kazhakstan.

Episode 6: **Three's Company**

▶ **Airdate: July 16, 2006** | **Directed by Ken Whittingham** | **Written by Lisa Alden**

On the heels of Vince's $20 million demand to do *A2*, the guys blow off some steam at a Hollywood hotspot. What was meant to be a boys' night out takes an unexpected turn when they bump into Sloan and her smoking-hot friend, Tori. While Turtle and Drama think that they have a shot with her, it's E that she really wants—in a threesome with Sloan. Vince, meanwhile, informs Ari that he's not taking his calls until Drama gets a job, but relents when Lloyd hooks Drama up with an audition for an Ed Burns pilot.

Episode 7: **Strange Days**

▶ **Airdate: July 23, 2006** | **Directed by Mark Mylod** | **Written by Marc Abrams & Michael Benson**

E goes to the Standard to apologize to Tori after waking up snuggling her, and not his girlfriend, Sloan. Meanwhile, Ari is caught in his own compromising position when rival Adam Davies spies him and Mrs. Ari emerging from the new office space Ari hopes to turn into his new agency, using the $11 million severance from Terrance. Sloan talks Vince into putting himself up for bid in her charity auction, but Vince winds up talking a hot waitress into putting an end to the bidding early.
▶ Before acting as mortal enemies on *Entourage*, Connolly and guest star Seth Green starred in a commercial for Matchbox together in 1982. Ellin thought that Green was "so freaking funny," he reworked the Vegas episode to include him.

Episode 8: **The Release**

▶ Airdate: July 30, 2006 | Directed by Patty Jenkins | Written by Brian Burns & Doug Ellin

Barbara Miller sandbags Ari when their lunch is actually a surprise meeting with the heads of the major agencies in Hollywood. There, Terrance tells Ari that he won't sign any of his severance checks to fund Ari's huge new agency. But Barbara steps in to save Ari's dream by funding the agency in exchange for partnership. In all the excitement, no one at Ari's agency picks up Vince's calls before he and Billy Walsh sabotage the opening of the now-colorized *Queens Boulevard*. Drama lands a role in the Eddie Burns pilot *Five Towns*. ▶ Brian Burns had to find the perfect reason for his brother Ed to guest on the show, which he says had a hometown spin. "Me, Rob [Weiss], and my brother are from this part of Long Island called the five towns, so it was kind of just a cool setting for the type of show that Eddie would do."

Episode 9: **Vegas Baby, Vegas!**

Airdate: August 6, 2006 | Directed by Julian Farino | Written by Doug Ellin

Turtle hooks up a Vegas weekend for Vince and the guys, complete with a hundred grand payday for Vince to judge a stripper contest. They kidnap Ari, who goes halves with Vince on his gambling, but regrets it early on when Vince goes down big. E's got issues of his own, with Seth Green insinuating that he has a past with Sloan. Drama is rubbed the wrong way by a masseur mistaking Drama's admiration for a come-on. ▶ While taking breaks from shooting, Jerry Ferrara continued his onscreen luck offscreen by taking home nearly $10,000 in winnings.

Episode 10: **I Wanna Be Sedated**

Airdate: August 13, 2006 | **Directed by Julian Farino** | **Written by Doug Ellin & Lisa Alden**

With Vince chilling with a cute girl at Book Soup—and then a hotel room—E heads to the new Miller Gold Agency to meet with Ari. Busy with company issues, Ari sets E up with Bob Ryan, an ancient producer who is bugging Ari for a star for his next flick. After what proves to be a miserable day, Bob surprises E with an old script he has based on Joey Ramone's life. It's also Turtle's big record-signing day with Saigon. When Saigon doesn't show up for the label meeting, Turtle and Drama try to track him down room-to-room at the Standard. ➔ Ellin actually based the character of Bob Ryan on a producer from his second feature, *Kissing a Fool*, who inspired the catchphrase "Is that something you might be interested in?

Episode 11: **What About Bob?**

▶ **Airdate: August 20, 2006** | **Directed by Ken Whittingham** | **Written by Brian Burns**

While running the Hollywood studio gauntlet to pitch *I Wanna Be Sedated* with E, Ari ditches Bob Ryan and gets a sweet deal from Universal. Bob has the last word by selling it on his own to Warner Bros. Vince takes Turtle to score some rare sneakers designed by graffiti artist Fukijama, but he refuses to use his celebrity status to cut the line. After a frantic trip to Santa Monica, where they miss out again, Vince has the artist create a one-of-a-kind pair. Drama's worrying about his monologue in *Five Towns*, but Turtle's handy stress relief advice saves the day.

Episode 12: **Sorry, Ari**

▶ **Airdate: August 27, 2006** | **Directed by Julian Farino** | **Written by Doug Ellin & Rob Weiss**

After the Ramones project falls apart, Vince is thinking seriously about switching agents. The guys take meetings around town, but they're all putting on the same dog-and-pony show and the guys are unimpressed. Ari's plan to save the Ramones project for Vince backfires and costs Vince any chance of getting the role. E and Vince give Ari and the Miller Gold Agency one last shot to win them back, but Ari gives the same lame presentation as all of the other agencies, and this, along with his inability to say sorry, gets him fired.

Episode 13: **Less Than 30**

▶ **Airdate: April 8, 2007** | **Directed by Julian Farino** | **Written by Doug Ellin**

With Ari no longer in the picture, Vince has moved onto a new agent, the stunning Amanda. Turtle tries to figure out a way to throw Vince's birthday party on the Queen Mary under budget. Ari, meanwhile, isn't about to go away that quietly. His gift to Vince? The *Medellin* script, which Ari insists is back in play.

Episode 14: **Dog Day Afternoon**

▶ **Airdate: April 15, 2007** | **Directed by Mark Mylod** | **Written by Doug Ellin & Rob Weiss**

When Eric wants to go to wine country with Sloan, Vince suggests coming along, promising to find a "travel-worthy" date. Sloan accuses E of being unable to say no to Vince. Turtle and Drama find girls of their own at the dog park, but Ahnold takes a chomp out of the girls' dog back at the house. Ari uses Lloyd as bait to sign mega TV writer Jay Lester. When Lester takes a shine to Lloyd, Ari hightails it to Boys' Town to avoid literally pimping out his assistant.

Episode 15: **Manic Monday**

▶ **Airdate: April 22, 2007** | **Directed by Julian Farino** | **Written by Doug Ellin & Marc Abrams & Michael Benson**

Vince discovers the problem with having a hot-looking agent is never being able to say no, while Ari is having a hard time letting go. After tearing up at the sight of Vince on his screensaver, Ari crashes his shrink's golf course for an emergency session. Ari regains his mojo by firing the optically- and competency-challenged Rob Rubino. Vince also decides to solve his problem with Amanda by confessing to her that he thinks she's cute.

Episode 16: **Gotcha!**

▶ **Airdate: April 29, 2007** | **Directed by Daniel Attias** | **Written by Doug Ellin & Rob Weiss**

When Drama finds out he's going to be on Pauly Shore's hidden camera show, *Gotcha!*, he accidentally slights UFC Champ Chuck Lidell, drawing the wrath of the ultimate fighter. Ari's one-time loser frat brother Scott comes to stay with the Golds, but Ari is annoyed to learn that Scott is a dot-com millionaire with a Perfect Ten fiancée. E deals with finding out that Vince is hooking up with Amanda, and that it might be more than a one-time deal.

⊘ **ARTIE LANGE**

Listeners of *The Howard Stern Show* have been hearing actor/comedian/radio personality Artie Lange's toe-curling tales of drunken-and-drugged-out debauchery for years. So it came as a bit of a surprise to see him play against type in Season 3 as Scott Siegel, Ari's old fraternity brother, a reformed party animal who made $90 million off an Internet endeavor and shows up with his beautiful, young blond fiancé, which sends the always-competitive Ari into a crisis about his own personal and professional success.

Did you and Jeremy Piven do any improvisation on the episode?
Yeah. He liked to just roll with it, you know, which was fine with me. I did mostly standup, but I did some improv back in New York City. And I had met Jeremy really, really briefly on the set of *Old School*. In our episode, there's the scene where we're having lunch by the pool and he said, "At the end, I'm just going to add a couple of insults like maybe I used to insult you in college." And I was like, "That's great." And Doug Ellin said, "But now you're a little more confident, so if Ari does that, feel free to talk back to him." So at the end, he improvs, "You've got a face only a mother could love." And I said, "Yeah, your mother loves it." It just sort of rolled off my tongue and they yelled "cut." It probably wasn't right for the character, but the whole crew cracked up, which was cool.

Episode 17: **Return of the King**

▶ Airdate: May 6, 2007 | **Directed by Daniel Attias** | **Written by Brian Burns**

Yom Kippur is meant to be a day of atonement, but there is no rest for Ari when *Medellin* producer Nick Rubenstein informs him that Benicio Del Toro has dropped out and he wants Vince to play Pablo Escobar. Nicky and Ari try to land Vince before the sun goes down. At the racetrack with the guys, Vince gets the news and is thrilled, but he gets concerned when it appears Amanda is dragging her feet. Drama's favorite horse, King's Ransom, comes up lame, but Drama buys "the King" and takes the big fella home.

Episode 18: **The Resurrection**

▶ Airdate: May 13, 2007 | **Directed by David Nutter** | **Written by Doug Ellin & Ally Musika**

It's the day of the *Five Towns* series premiere, but negative reviews send Drama into a tailspin. As a premiere gift, Vince gets Drama's '65 Lincoln convertible all fixed up, and in the process Turtle meets Kelly, the sneaker-loving girl of his dreams. Meanwhile, Vince and E set their sights on pulling *Medellin* out of turnaround. Ari enlists the help of mega-producer Joe Roberts, who will pick up *Medellin* only if Vince lowers himself to star in *Matterhorn*. Vince comes up with another solution: buy *Medellin* himself. Now all he has to do is sell his mansion.

Episode 19: **The Prince's Bride**

▶ **Airdate: May 20, 2007** | **Directed by David Nutter** | **Written by Rob Weiss**

Now that *Medellin* is the property of Vince and E, Ari lines up shadowy producer Yair Marx to finance it. Yair is up for it, as long as Vince is up for sleeping with the financier's wife. Lloyd sends Drama up to Brett Ratner's house to audition for *Rush Hour 3*. Turns out Ratner misread the credits and didn't want Drama after all, but the actor who plays his kid brother on the show. Turtle's date with Kelly is interrupted by her overprotective father. ▶ Ratner was nervous about the gig, knowing he'd follow in the footsteps of James Cameron and Paul Haggis. "I said, 'I'm not a good actor.' I was freaked out. Doug goes, 'Don't worry, you'll be great.' He and Rob Weiss and I got together and we spent a lot of time hanging out. And it was just great."

Episode 20: **Adios Amigos**

▶ Airdate: June 3, 2007 | **Directed by Mark Mylod** | **Written by Doug Ellin**

When Nick Rubenstein's trust fund kicks in, he decides to sink his cash into funding *Medellin* himself. Vince and E are tasked with finding a director and turn to *Queens Boulevard* director Billy Walsh. They find Billy shooting porn in the Valley under the pseudonym Wally Balls. Walsh reads and loves the script, but, weary of Hollywood suits monkeying around with his films, he demands final cut. Meanwhile, Drama decides it's time to move out and looks for a condo of his own.

success and excess
the many perks of living the life ›››

TURTLE:

FRIENDS ARE JUST GIRLS YOU HAVEN'T FUCKED YET, E. YOU KNOW THAT.

EMILY

ARI: That's why no more guys. You fire a guy, you create a rival. You fire a woman and you create a housewife.

Hot Girl on Sidewalk

CASSIE

DRAMA: CASSIE, HOW YOU DOIN'? PEACE CORPS, HUH? WHERE YOU GONNA BE STATIONED?

CASSIE: UH, THE SUDAN.

TURTLE: THOSE ARE SOME LUCKY SUDANERS.

Turtle:
Ten bucks, but you give me your phone number, it's five.

FLYER GIRL

Staci

JUSTINE CHAPIN

Ari: Justine Chapin. Every young actor in Hollywood wants to be the first one in there, man. Take a number.
Eric: What kind of virgin has a snake tat pointin' down to their box?

Fiona

MARISSA
THE MOTORCYCLE MODEL

BRETT:
WHY ARE THERE DOUGHNUTS HERE? I DON'T UNDERSTAND. THESE ARE SUPERMODELS NOT TEAMSTERS.

SLOAN

ERIC: So your dad is pretty good with a gun.

SLOAN: You should see him with a crossbow.

ERIC: You serious?

SLOAN: Oh, yeah. He's great with all weapons and he's even better with his bare knuckles.

DRAMA: I THOUGHT THAT MAYBE A LITTLE KISS MIGHT ADD SOME PATHOS.
BROOKE: KISS?
DRAMA: YEAH, NOTHING CRAZY, MORE IN LOVE THAN LUST.
BROOKE: YOU'RE PLAYING MY BROTHER.
DRAMA: REALLY? I DIDN'T EVEN GET A FULL SCRIPT. YOUR BROTHER. THAT WOULD BE WEIRD.

BROOKE SHIELDS

MARIA MENOUNOS
BIG MOVIE, YOU LOOK HANDSOME.

Sundance Publicists Corinne and Jen

Tory

Li Lei

SHEILA JAFFE ➔ Casting Director

I'll tell you what's the toughest part to cast on this show—which you wouldn't think is tough in L.A. Every episode has a hot blond girl in it. Guys may think that there are all these hot blonds out here that can act. But trust me. They're hard to find. I mean, you get a picture of a girl and you think, Oh my God, she's a hot blonde, and then she walks in the room and you realize that the picture is from, you know, like five, ten years ago. It's like Johnny Drama's old headshot. It's crazy.

I've taken to telling my trainer in the gym to keep an eye out for girls. There's a bunch of guys on this show, so everybody has a different image of what hot is. And that's how it's usually written in the script. "Hot girl." Over the seasons, it has gone from "hot girl," to "supremely hot girl," "exquisitely hot girl," and "ridiculously hot girl." They now give me adverbs to the adjectives, so I'll really understand what they're after.

CHRISTY
SHAUNA'S ASSISTANT

CHRISTY: I'd never go out with you, Turtle.
TURTLE: If you ever need anything, y'know, concert tickets, pedicure, full body massage . . .
CHRISTY: How about a stun gun?

Amanda

WAITRESS: You seem like a hot ticket tonight.
VINCE: I feel like an iPod. Hey, will you buy me?
WAITRESS: I don't think I could afford you.
VINCE: I could loan you the money.

LINDSAY
THE COCKTAIL WAITRESS

DRAMA:
SHE GAVE ME THE RIDE OF MY LIFE. I JUST HUNG ONTO THOSE LATS, SURRENDERED ALL CONTROL.

TANYA DRAMA'S MUSCLE GIRLFRIEND

Jessica Alba

Mandy Moore

VINCE (TO JIMMY KIMMEL):

We just had sex about five minutes ago.

SARA FOSTER

Nika Marx

TURTLE: Wow. All these years I been wondering where girls hide during the day.

DRAMA: And true dog people know that a Rot's tough exterior's merely a protective shell that hides a wealth of sensitivity they have within.

DOG WALKER GIRLS
ALLYSON AND CHERYL

PORN ACTRESS MONIQUE ALEXANDER

PORN STAR: I never did two guys before.
VINCE: Uh, there's a first time for everything, right?
PORN STAR: I guess

1

2

3

4

→ cameos

8

12

13

14

134

BOB
SAGET

You probably first met Bob Saget as the father on *Full House* or as the host of *America's Funniest Home Videos*, but in Season 2, Episode 5, he tweaks his wholesome image by appearing as a prostitute-loving, dope-smoking, self-obsessed-even-by-Hollywood-standards neighbor. Armed with a muffin basket and—what else?—a collection of *Full House* DVDs, he heads over to welcome the boys to the block, and to find out just who's more famous—Vince or him.

ARE YOU MORE LIKE YOUR *ENTOURAGE* CHARACTER OR YOUR *FULL HOUSE* CHARACTER? I'm probably in between those characters depending on who I'm with. I mean, I have a nice house. I have a clean house. So that would make me like the *Full House* guy. But I'm not the one, you know, scrubbing it. I probably am like that *Entourage* character a little bit. He's not desperate. He loves his life. And I think that's why people love Jack Nicholson. So I was kind of playing that. But honestly, I wasn't playing that. I hate to say

it, but I do have that quality. Like I don't really watch my language that much around my kids. But I don't curse. It was not a stretch to act like that. I have acted like that, but I've never been that aggressively cocky and arrogant. WHAT'S THE ONE QUESTION FANS ALWAYS ASK YOU ABOUT THE EPISODE? Everybody wants to know about the house of hookers. These guys all go, "Where is that house?" I'm like, "Dude, what are you talking about?" It's a house in the Palisades that they rented and they put girls in bikinis in it. It's supposed to be the Heidi Fleiss kind of thing and I don't know if that house exists, but I've never seen it. WHAT'S THE ONE LINE PEOPLE REMEMBER FROM THE CAMEO? I'll walk out onstage and people will yell at me, "Don't you fuck my daughters!" And I'll go, "Please, please stop that." I just tell them to shut up, don't talk about my daughters. And they love that because I'm just being real. WHAT'S UP WITH THE CRAZY HANDSHAKE WITH TURTLE? I have a problem with that, by the way. I have a real stupid, awkward, Jewish, white-guy problem in that if people feel to me like they're more

from the street, more of a homeboy, I will do these handshakes. I don't want to do them, and I'm not forcing it. I'm not trying to be white-guy cool boy. I just couldn't help it. He was standing by the door and I just wanted to say good-bye to him in a respectful way—the way you would say good-bye to Turtle.

For many fans, nothing quite lifts the human spirit

as the moment in Season 3 when the boys band together to defend Sloan's honor and give actor Seth Green and his posse of posers a Queens-style beat-down they will never forget. After all, the tension had been building since Green first appeared in Season 3, Episode 7 at the pool on top of the Standard, where he taunts Eric about his past with Sloan. The mind games continue in Las Vegas (Season 3, Episode 9) where they run into each other again. It all comes to a head at the Hard Rock and ends in a glorious bar brawl. While Green and E may be mortal enemies on the show, in real life, they've actually been good pals for a long time.

memorable line
"I must have been dreaming how I blasted her in the face like a Jackson Pollock."

IS IT TRUE THAT YOU DID A MATCHBOX COMMERCIAL WITH KEVIN CONNOLLY WHEN YOU WERE KIDS? Yeah! Kevin and I, we've known each other forever. I ran into him and I told him how much I loved the show, and he said that they had talked about me coming on and doing a little bit and was I open to that. And I said of course I was. SO HOW DID THE SLOAN IDEA COME UP? Doug Ellin had this Vegas episode planned, and this is what Kevin had talked to me about initially—would I be opposed to playing kind of an A-hole version of myself? And I said, based on my reputation, I think it'd be funny. I mean, everything I've ever heard about me is that I'm exceedingly nice, which is a great reputation to have. And it's fun to be able to play a jerky version of yourself. And I said, I'd love to do something silly like that. So I came and did that one bit on the roof of the Downtown Standard. And when I was there, I talked a bunch with Doug Ellin about the possibility of doing this other bit, and we just spent a ton of time that day having fun and being silly together, and kind of set up within that scene the possibility that maybe Eric and Seth Green have history. SO WHAT REALLY HAPPENED BETWEEN YOU AND SLOAN? What we decided was that we

SETH GREEN

had known each other when we were teenagers and she'd had kind of a weak moment wherein I seduced her—we were like fifteen—and it was one time and she always regretted it. But I lorded it over her like I was the cock of the walk. So every time we've seen each other since, I'm like, "Hey, how ya doing? Good to see you. You miss it?" YOU HAVE A JACKED-UP ENTOURAGE ON THE SHOW. WHO ARE THOSE CLOWNS? Well, one of the guys was a PA on the show. He was just somebody that everybody liked that works behind the scenes and they gave him a part. And then the other kid was cast locally. He was just in Vegas for the weekend and they paid his hotel to stay for the rest of the week and be in the scene. He was just a funny, tough guy. TELL US ABOUT THE INFAMOUS "JACKSON POLLOCK" LINE? Doug Ellin actually had to go and shoot something else and I begged them to give me a B camera just to run off a bunch of ideas. And they literally just had a camera set up in front of me. The other cast members weren't even there, it was just me and a bunch of extras. And I just fired off like seven or eight options. But the Jackson Pollock line I liked because it implied a certain amount of sophisticated sleaziness.

138

RALPH
MA
CCHI
O

Who let the chimps out? In Drama's mind, it was none other than the Karate Kid, Mr. Ralph Macchio, who cameos in Season 2, Episode 3. One night, about a decade ago, as Drama tells the boys, he and Ralph were at the Playboy Mansion together, hanging out near The Grotto, sucking back shots of Cuervo, and "The next thing I know, he's standing in the Miyagi crane position, kicking the cage wide open." Later, Johnny Chase was banned from the Mansion for life. So when the guys head into the den of decadence for a party without him, Drama scales the wall and confronts Macchio, who fights back, calling Drama an "ex–evening soap star." Turns out, neither of them was Hef's "monkey boy." But Drama and Macchio have way more in common than you might think.

YOU AND KEVIN DILLON GO WAY BACK, RIGHT? Yeah. I worked with his brother, Matt, on *The Outsiders* and I've known Kevin since the early '80s. I know the whole Dillon clan, and they're from the East Coast as well. And so I just thought it made sense to be involved with his character. It just seemed right. YOU HAVE A CONNECTION TO THE CHARACTER OF DRAMA AS WELL. I auditioned for that role. I came and I auditioned for it and I did fine, you know? I could see why it made sense to bring me in, because I sort of was popular in the day and not as popular now, so it would be kind of fun to play that. But when I heard they got Kevin, I'm like, "Now that's it," because he plays everything so straight and real. He's so desperate and pathetic, but yet charming and adorable at the same time. IN THE EPISODE, YOUR WIFE WASN'T SO HOT ABOUT YOU HANGING OUT AT HEF'S. WHAT DID YOUR WIFE REALLY THINK ABOUT YOUR FILMING AT THE MANSION? I asked my wife if I could shoot a day at the Playboy Mansion and she was like, "Please, get out of the house. Get out and do something." We've been married long enough, she's like, "Go!" You know, maybe when we were first married, it would've been tough to put that one by. Two kids, married close to twenty years, and now she's like, "You know what? I'll drive you there." WHAT KIND OF REACTION DID YOU GET FROM YOUR APPEARANCE ON *ENTOURAGE*? All of a sudden, I became a good actor because it's something that the industry found cool, you know? The morning after the show aired was really a testament to what happens when a show is industry-savvy or is in the consciousness of the Hollywood industry. I mean, I could've done three episodes on *CSI*, the number-one show in the country at the time, and I wouldn't have gotten the response the next morning as I did being on *Entourage*, when everybody in L.A. is watching it.

Talk about Gary Busey's two episodes on *Entourage*

and one word comes up over and over again: spontaneity. It was "spontaneity" that inspired him to repeatedly tackle Kevin Connolly between takes and tickle him. It was that same free-spirited outlook that made him try to ban Stephen Levinson from setting foot on the set. But nowhere did his unconstrained nature come out more than in the acting itself. Knowing his reputation for improvisation, Doug Ellin turned Busey loose without a script. Yep, not a single word was written down for either his turn as an artist having a debut of modern paintings and sculptures (one of which Turtle knocks over), or his subsequent appearance as a beach-bum philosopher. And the results: As his character said, "I don't think there's a word in the Earth language or in the dictionary to define what it did to me." But here are a few of the hightlights.

ON HIS PLANS FOR TURTLE

GARY BUSEY → I could snap your sternum with one blow from my forehead to your chest. I could raise my head up and loosen your teeth, knock you down, grab you by the lip, pull you up, and tell you "I'll be right back." While we're here, we're all lookin' for the art within ourselves. Gravity, inertia, and physics. It's like a round robin.

GARY BUSEY → I'm cleansing you in the name of art and everything art stands for. Remember this—art is only the search. It's not the final form.

ON HIS FEELINGS TOWARD ARI

GARY BUSEY → I know you. You are a gut-maggot with no guts. **ARI →** And you're gonna spin off this planet. I love it. Keep at it.

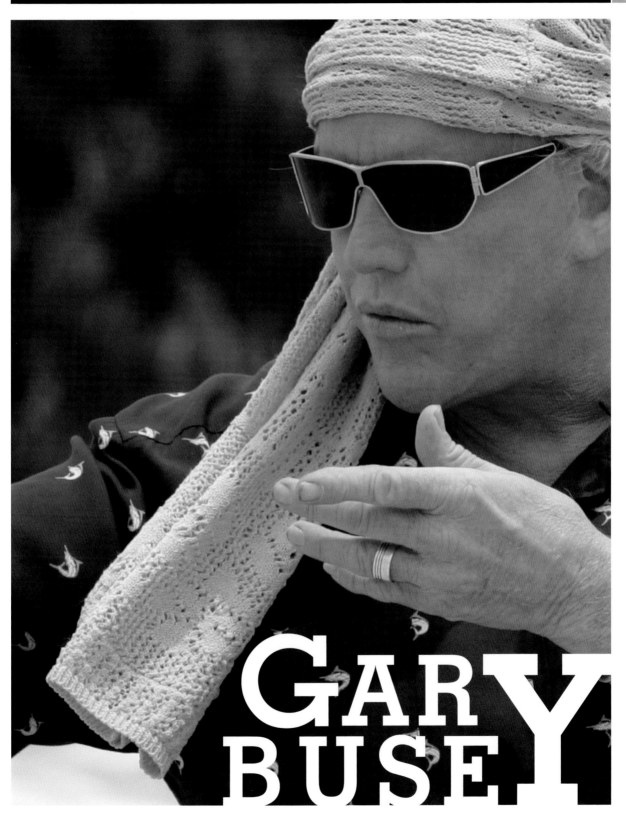

GARY BUSEY

GUEST STARS

Even when they're not playing a version of themselves, the celebrities are flocking to *Entourage*. From legends like Martin Landau, Mercedes Ruehl, and Malcolm McDowell to up-and-comers like Bai Ling and Rainn Wilson, *Entourage* never comes up short when it comes to big names.

① Timothy Busfield as the director of the Movie of the Week that Johnny Drama did not get to make with Brooke Shields. ② Sophie Vergara plays Vince's leading lady in *Medellin*, but it's director Billy Walsh who falls hard for her. ③ Domenick Lombardozzi as Dom, Shrek-stealing friend from the old neighborhood. ④ Paul Ben-Victor, as lying Warner Bros. head. ⑤ Nora Dunn, as patient couple's therapist to the Golds. ⑥ Bryan Callen, as optically-challenged agent Rob Rubino. ⑦ Maury Chaykin as movie heavyweight Harvey Weingard. ⑧ Adam Goldberg as heir and aspiring producer Nick Rubenstein. ⑨ Carla Gugino as agent and love-interest to Vince, Amanda. ⑩ Martin Landau as somewhat-senile-but-still-kicking producer Bob Ryan. ⑪ Mercedes Ruehl as Vince's flight-phobic mom. ⑫ Malcolm McDowell as Terrance McQuewick, arch-nemesis and former Ari Gold boss. ⑬ Bai Ling as irresistible stunt coordinator Lei Ling. ⑭ Rainn Wilson as intrepid and influential Internet reporter, R. J. Spencer.

Episode Guide
Season 4 : Exaltation

Episode 1: **Welcome to the Jungle**

▶ **Airdate: June 17, 2007** | **Directed by Mark Mylod** | **Written by Doug Ellin**

Vince and E have finally landed their dream project, *Medellin*, but shooting it in Colombia with director Billy Walsh is a nightmare. To make matters worse, a documentary crew has tagged along to capture the action. Eric is charged with maintaining the budget, and his crew's sanity—no easy task when the director has fallen for his female lead and outlaws sex on the set. Walsh also demands more money for a Stephen Gaghan rewrite. On top of that, Ari has his doubts that first-time producers Eric and Vince can pull off the multimillion-dollar production, and Drama attempts to parlay the success of his NBC show, *Five Towns*, into a role in *Medellin*.

144

Episode 2: **The First Cut is the Deepest**

▶ **Airdate: June 24, 2007** | **Directed by Mark Mylod** | **Written by Doug Ellin**

After the grueling shoot in Colombia and a relaxing three months in Italy, Billy Walsh summons E and Vince back to Hollywood to screen the first cut of *Medellin*. When the time comes for them to watch the film, a suddenly self-conscious Walsh bolts on his motorcycle with the reel tucked under his arm, leading the guys on a chase through the underbelly of L.A. Turtle wants to plan a killer "Welcome Home" party for Vince at Drama's new apartment, but Drama, to ensure his pad is not harmed, institutes a strict "No Buffalo Wings" policy, padlocks his bathroom door, and rents portable toilets for the guests. Meanwhile, Ari runs into an unexpected roadblock when trying to get his son into an exclusive private school.

Episode 3: **Malibooty**

▶ Airdate: July 1, 2007 | Directed by Ken Whittingham | Written by Rob Weiss

Eric, disappointed with the first cut of *Medellin*, has notes for Billy Walsh, but Walsh is not the kind of director who listens to anyone—nor does he have to, seeing as he has final cut. The only way for E to wrestle back control is by selling *Medellin* to a distributor. E's plight is compounded when he learns that Walsh submitted their film to the Cannes Film Festival. Ari finds Eric an unlikely business partner in Harvey Weingard. Drama and Turtle head up to Malibu to rendezvous with Drama's one-time lust object, Donna Devaney, and her friend Marjorie. While Marjorie hasn't aged as gracefully as Donna, she tries to make up for it by being a full-service date. Vince, meanwhile, tries to get lucky with a Malibu hottie—and Dennis Hopper.

Episode 4: **Sorry, Harvey**

▶ Airdate: July 8, 2007 | Directed by Ken Whittingham | Written by Doug Ellin

Drama's loving his new condo, but hating its Los Angeles zip code. Drama enlists his baby bro to convince the mayor of Beverly Hills to annex Drama's building. The mayor offers a counterproposal—if the guys can get him laid, Drama's condo is 90210. A valet mixes Ari's Lexus Hybrid up with M. Night Shyamalan's same car, and Ari has to go all the way to Oxnard—far out of his comfort zone—to retrieve a top-secret script that he left in his car. Eric also goes outside of his comfort zone at a dinner with Harvey Weingard, a supposedly reformed rage-aholic, by rescinding on his deal to sell Harvey *Medellin*.

Episode 5: **The Dream Team**

▶ **Airdate: July 15, 2007** | **Directed by Seith Mann** | **Written by Brian Burns**

When the *Medellin* trailer hits YouTube without Billy Walsh's authorization, Billy accuses Eric of leaking it. Eric stands his ground when the arguing and name-calling turns into an all-out brawl at Barney Greengrass. Billy obviously didn't see the upshot of having the hottest trailer on the Internet, as the "Dream Team" of Vince, Eric, and Walsh becomes Hollywood's most in-demand filmmaking team overnight. Ari maneuvers and manipulates old friends and fails to secure Vince and the crew *Lost In The Clouds*, a cool new project they want. And Drama, dying to be seen as cool on the *Five Towns* set, lies his way into a medical marijuana prescription, but shows his age when trying to hang with his young castmates in a game of "Strip or Smoke."

Episode 6: **The WeHoHo**

▶ Airdate: July 22, 2007 | Directed by Mark Mylod | Written by Doug Ellin

Ari's attempts to close the *Lost in the Clouds* deal are suspended when a distraught Lloyd takes a leave of absence. What's his problem? Seems his boyfriend, Tom, broke up with him because he's working too much. But if anyone knows that things aren't always what they seem it's Ari, as he finds out when he tracks down Lloyd's ex. Meanwhile, E's having reservations about another go-round with Billy Walsh and his filmmaker-from-hell routine on *Clouds*. Turtle and Drama take a day trip to Palmdale to see about a moneymaking scheme Turtle's cousin cooked up involving an ailing baseball legend.

Episode 7: **The Day F*ckers**

▶ Airdate: July 29, 2007 | Directed by Mark Mylod | Written by Rob Weiss

Who says Eric can't have unemotional sex? Drama, for one. In fact, Drama is so convinced of it that he bets Vince five grand Turtle can find and close a no-strings-attached daytime fling before E can. Vince takes E under his wing for the day, but Eric's progress with a British stunner is halted when E runs into Sloan. Turtle's adventure starts out promising when he meets a smoking hot blonde, but things get a little too furry, even for an animal like Turtle. Ari takes drastic measures to ensure that his son, Jonah, doesn't wind up in the sleeper cell that is Los Angeles public elementary school.

147

Episode 8: **Gary's Desk**

▶ **Airdate: August 5, 2007** | **Directed by Julian Farino** | **Written by Ally Musika**

Eric just rented an office, if it can be called that. It's in a shabby building in Hollywood and has an old card table in lieu of a desk. While E tries to get the word out that his company, The Murphy Group, is up and running, the guys head out in search of a man's desk for E, a trip that lands them in Gary Busey's art studio. At Miller Gold, Ari readies the agency for a visit from Mary J. Blige, but infidelity and infighting between twin brother agents brings more drama than Ari can handle.

Episode 9: **The Young and the Stoned**

▶ **Airdate: August 12, 2007** | **Directed by Mark Mylod** | **Written by Dusty Kay**

Having received an advance check for *Lost in the Clouds*, Vince and the guys are finally able to move out of Drama's condo. On his way up to their new house, Eric gets into a fender bender with a towel-clad Anna Faris. Eric manages to turn the awkward situation into a date that night, but the guys question whether Eric's romantic interest in Anna will be reciprocated. Turtle picks up three girls while shopping for a feast, but they may prove more trouble than they're worth. When Ari learns that his wife is slated to have a make-out scene in her return to *The Young and the Restless*, no mode of sabotage is too sleazy or underhanded for the superagent.

148

Episode 10: **Snow Job**

▶ **Airdate: August 19, 2007** | **Directed by Ken Whittingham** | **Written by Doug Ellin & Ally Musika**

Despite having different intentions than Anna Faris the previous night, Eric, with Vince's blessing, agrees to manage her. E is called down to help Anna at a photoshoot, but has to contend with her loser boyfriend's jealousy. Meanwhile, Vince receives the first draft of *Lost in the Clouds* from Billy Walsh, except instead of snowy mountains, it's set on a post-apocalyptic farm. Now Ari has to convince the studio that the snowless script, *Silo*, is worthy of the greenlight.

Episode 11: **No Cannes Do**

▶ **Airdate: August 26, 2007** | **Directed by Dan Attias** | **Written by Doug Ellin & Rob Weiss**

The guys are off to Cannes with Ari and Billy Walsh for the world premiere of *Medellin*. The only problem is getting there, seeing how a terror threat at LAX has delayed all flights. While Ari looks for alternate means of air travel, and Turtle and Drama try to smoke out potential terrorists at the airport, Billy and Vince see the extra time in L.A. as a chance to sit down with E's client, Anna Faris, and discuss a role for her in *Silo*. Eric doesn't think the project is a good fit for Anna, but Vince pressures E to sell her on the movie. When E cracks under pressure and confesses to Anna he doesn't like *Silo*, he winds up blowing his chances with Anna for a romantic or professional future.

Episode 12: **The Cannes Kids**

▶ **Airdate: September 2, 2007** | **Directed by Mark Mylod** | **Written by Doug Ellin**

The boys have arrived at the Cannes Film Festival and *Medellin* is the hottest film in competition. Upon entering their hotel, the guys are approached by Yair Marx, who invites them to a party. With Nick Rubenstein barking orders from L.A., Yair makes an offer for *Medellin* to be the first film distributed under his new company. Ari uses the deal to bring Dana Gordon into the bidding war. Meanwhile, Drama, a huge star in France, wins over a gorgeous *Viking Quest* fan, but loses her when he gets kicked out of the hotel.

RHYS COIRO ON PLAYING UNCOMPROMISING AUTEUR BILLY WALSH, DIRECTOR OF *QUEENS BOULEVARD* AND *MEDELLIN*.

I've said to myself before how I wish in certain situations I could be more like Billy Walsh. He's dogmatic. He's a negotiator. He gets things done. He's a great doer of things. He's a hardnosed workman. And that's fun. You know, he's completely indefatigable; he quickly forgets any chinks in his armor that are revealed on the show.

There really wasn't any explanation about the character being based on [*Entourage* executive producer] Rob Weiss, but the understanding was that it was Rob. When I first came in to do the character, Rob was there as a consultant. I was fairly new to Hollywood when I first started playing the role. He's based on an amalgamation of family members and people that I know. But I didn't base him on any actual directors. I don't know too many directors, fortunately.

Mike Davis, transportation coordinator for *Entourage*, knows that in Los Angeles, you are what you drive. Don't believe it? Just try tossing the keys to your '78 Pinto to the valet at The Grill and see how that goes for you. Davis spends his days thinking up the perfect car for each character and scenario (along with the show's producers, of course), then begging, borrowing, or just flat-out buying it for the show. Take Turtle's Yellow Hummer. "That's got his name all over it," says Davis. Ditto for Sloan's Porche Cayenne, or the boys' everyday Escalade. Even E's 1988 Honda Prelude has history— executive producer Stephen Levinson once owned one when he first starting representing Mark Wahlberg. More than simply a status symbol, each car on *Entourage* is specifically selected to be a four-wheel extension of a character's personality and their perceived power in town. ⬇

Mercedes-Benz

HUMMER

DUCATI

LINCOLN

Eric:
Holy shit. You bought another hundred thousand dollar car, you sick maniac?

Vince:
No. It's not for me. It's for you.

DRAMA: You can't roll chicks on a Vespa, bro'.

MANAGER: When you drive a Rolls Royce, you are making a statement.

ERIC: And how expensive is this statement?

MANAGER: Three hundred and twenty thousand.

TURTLE: Not bad.

MANAGER: But if you sign a picture for my daughter, I'll give it to you for three-nineteen.

TURTLE: Ah. How much if he bangs his daughter?

MANAGER: We have excellent terms on our lease.

VINCE: Whattaya think, E?

ERIC: I think it costs more than the houses we grew up in.

TURTLE: A fuckin' Subaru costs more than the houses we grew up in.

Sloan: I don't know if it's true, but my father told me he changed the numbers on his wife's Mercedes so she thinks she's driving around in a six hundred and really it's a five.

ERIC: I'm test-driving a new car.

ARI: Matchbox or Hot Wheels?

ERIC: Funny. Vince feels bad about givin' away my Maserati.

ARI: Wow. When my father gave away my car, I was forced to lose my virginity on the back of a moped.

TURTLE: Big day for E. Brand new Maserati and you're gonna pop your cherry tonight.

DRAMA: Yeah, you're gonna love it, E. I had an Italian sports car in '94. They're a delight.

TURTLE: You had a Fiat, Drama.

DRAMA: Italian nonetheless.

MARVIN: He wants artistic integrity? Then let him drive around in a Prius.

VINCE: Yo, this car makes driving fun. I might even get my license.

The smoggy San Fernando Valley might be "Hell's waiting room," according to Drama, but there's plenty of other prime real estate to choose from in the City of Angels. The major dilemma when deciding where to live in L.A. is eastside versus westside. Eastern enclaves like the trendy Silver Lake neighborhood tend to be populated by the shaggy-haired, white-belt, hipper-than-thou set. Head west of La Cienega Boulevard (the line of demarcation in the city) into chic spots like West Hollywood, Beverly Hills, and Santa Monica, and L.A. starts to look more and more like its glamorous TV reflection. What's a hot young movie star to do? If you're like Vince, you hire a high-priced real-estate broker. For the rest of us, feel free to consult this handy breakdown of some of the cooler neighborhoods in L.A. and what it means to live there ⬇

Malibu

Dweller
The summer home of the rich and famous.

The Vibe
A place to ride waves rather than make them.

West Hollywood

Dweller

Paparazzi-prone young Hollywood.

The Vibe

Happiness is always one club away.

Santa Monica

Dweller

Secure enough to be away from the scene.

The Vibe

Beach. Lawns. Fred Segal.

Hollywood Hills

Dweller

Mid-level movie star.

The Vibe

Exclusively insular.

It's a truth universally acknowledged that a single man of good fortune must be in want of the latest, greatest toys. We're not talking foosball here, though the gang probably played their share back in Queens. These days, Vinnie has taken fun to a whole new level, lavishing $75,000 Full Swing Golf simulators and Xboxes on his crew. That's just the small stuff—when life is really looking up, the guys can whip out their Aston Martins or Ducatis and head downtown to Ari's courtside Lakers seats. Ain't life grand? ⬇

playboy mansion

ARI TO HIS WIFE:
You know, Playboy Mansion, strip clubs, whorehouses, I go where the meetings are, alright? It's my fuckin' job.

.....

TURTLE:
You can go to the Mansion in Underoos and still get laid, Vince.

ERIC:
Yeah, and you could go wrapped in bearer bonds and still not get laid, Turtle. Put the fuckin' pajamas away.

TURTLE:
You tellin' me we're gonna live by the beach. This is sick. This is like Far Rockaway minus the crack whores.

malibu

dressing up

SHAUNA:
Fuck spontaneity.
Well dressed, well prepared.
That's what makes
you a star.

ERIC:
Have I ever said
no to Vegas?
TURTLE:
Be like saying
no to a blowjob.

vegas

airplane

ERIC:
You know, only a real asshole
would spend thirty thousand
on a flight when the whole
job's only paying him sixty.

158 Eat, Drink, Live the Lifestyle

The first rule of an entourage is trust your entourage. This means have someone in your group who is going to be advance scout and ID the most happening locations in any town before you touch down. If you want to hang with really hot women, you have to go to the best places. To help get you started on the right path, here is the *Entourage* guide to hotels, restaurants, gyms, bars, and clubs. If you get in, don't just stand there and gawk.

legend

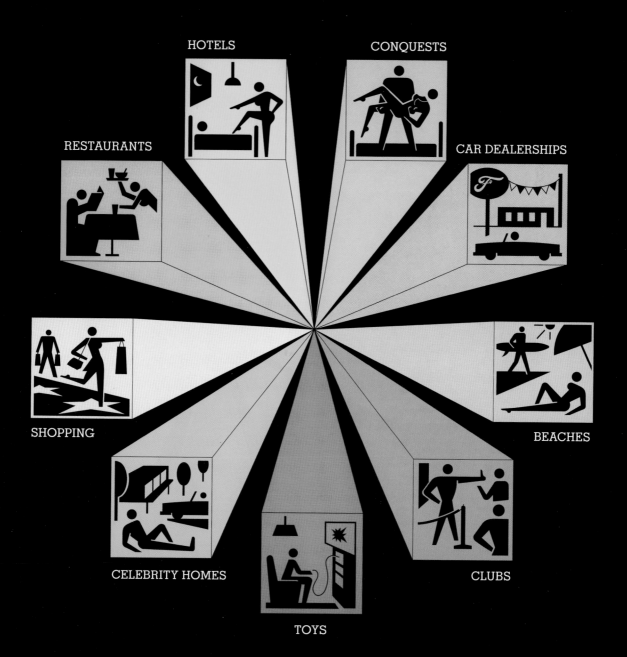

HOTELS

CONQUESTS

RESTAURANTS

CAR DEALERSHIPS

SHOPPING

BEACHES

CELEBRITY HOMES

CLUBS

TOYS

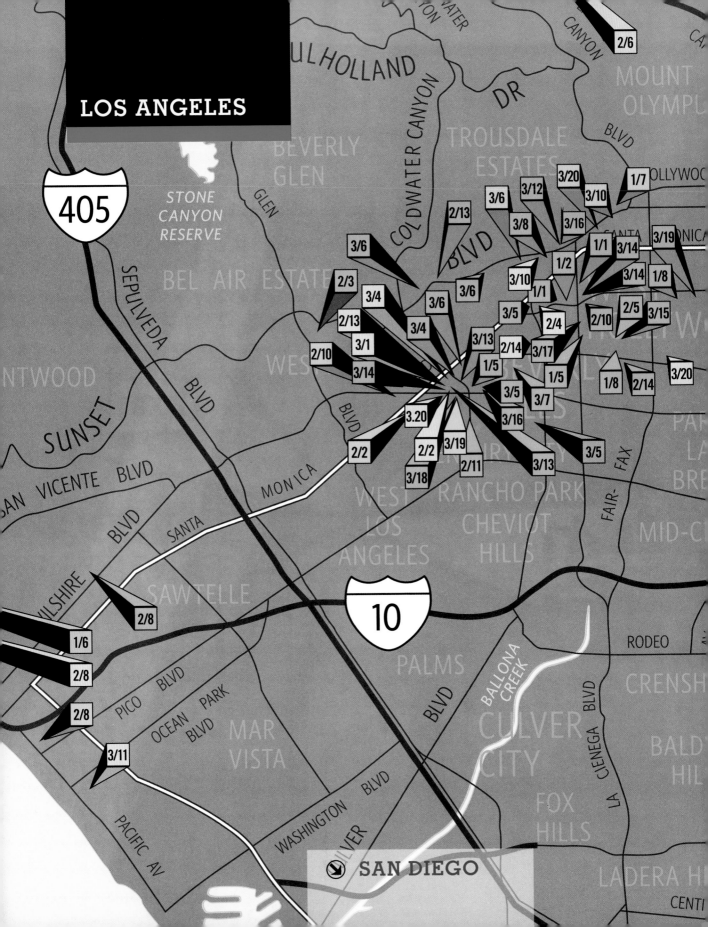

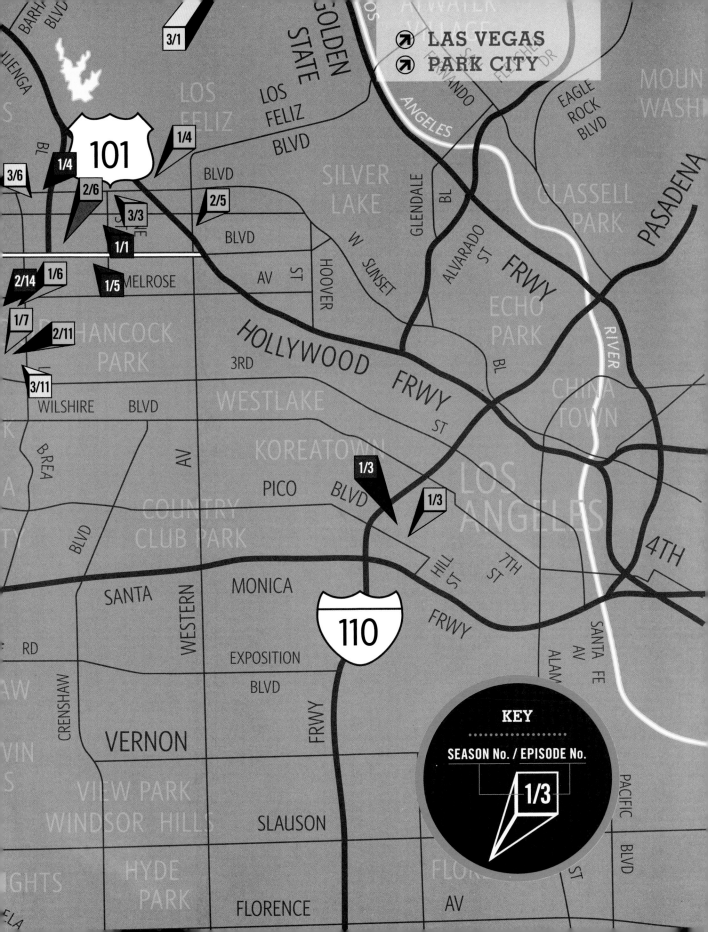

EPISODE 1: Pilot

MAURO'S CAFÉ & RISTORANTE

8112 Melrose Ave., West Hollywood (323.653.2874)

There's a reason why Doug Ellin chose to open the show's pilot episode with the boys eating lunch and tipping back Budweisers at Mauro's Café, located inside Fred Segal. "It's a great lunch spot where you can see lots of people," Ellin says. "Personally, I eat there twice a week.

ARCLIGHT HOLLYWOOD

6360 W. Sunset Blvd., Hollywood (323.464.1478)

Vince's *Head On* premiered at Hollywood's upscale ArcLight Hollywood cinemas (which is where *Entourage* hosts its own premieres). The theater houses fifteen screens (including the Cinerama Dome, a separate geodesic-shaped theater) as well as a bar and restaurant. Ticket prices are a bit higher than usual (around $14), but you get a lot of bang for your buck, including assigned seating, roomy chairs, an usher who introduces each film, "21 + screenings" where patrons can sip their favorite adult beverage, and concession stands that feature the best caramel corn in Los Angeles. The boys cruise back in Episode 4 to check out the crowds during *Head On's* opening weekend.

KOI

730 N. La Cienega Blvd., West Hollywood (310.659.9449)

Koi is the scene for several of Ari and E's power dinners. If you're lucky enough to get a reservation here (call early and often), sip sake martinis on the fire-lit patio, order the black cod bronzed with miso, and definitely bring your expense account.

URTH CAFFÉ

8565 Melrose Ave., West Hollywood
(310.659.0628)

Vince and the guys aren't the only famous folks who regularly trek to West Hollywood for Urth Caffé's organic coffees and food. Health-conscious celebrities have been seen hanging out on the terraced patio. Fight the mob of pretty people to place your order at the always-crowded counter and don't forget to try the tiramisu made with the café's own espresso. You can also visit the Santa Monica outpost at 2327 Main Street (near Hollister).

163

EPISODE 3: Talk Show

STAPLES CENTER

1111 S. Figueroa St., Downtown (213.742.7340)

The gang first hits the downtown sports arena for the Vitall Kitschko/Corrie Sanders fight and returns for a Los Angeles Lakers game in Season 2, Episode 2, sitting in the floor seats owned by the real Ari and enjoying the arena's members-only Grand Reserve Club, where they chat with hoops star Lamar Odom (with Drama asking about his calves) and Jaime Pressly, who invites them to a party at her beach house. They're back in Episode 17 for the U2 concert when Drama gets his b-day shout-out from Bono and again when Amanda gets Vince floor seats for Lakers/Golden State in Season 3, Episode 13.

THE PALM

1100 S. Flower St., Downtown (213.763.4600)

At this venerable downtown steak house during a real post-fight party, the boys chat up Luke Wilson (and get the home-entertainment-system hookup) and Jimmy Kimmel, an old pal of Drama's, who invites Vince to appear on the show. There is another location in Santa Monica, where Vince and E meet with studio chief Alan Grey in Season 3, Episode 5.

EPISODE 4: Date Night

LUCKY STRIKE LANES ➔

6801 Hollywood Blvd., Suite 143, Hollywood
(323.467.7776)

Neon-lit lanes and plasma-TV scoreboards make
this spot a must-visit for any hard-core, ten-pin fan.
The wooden bar top is actually lane sixteen from the
once-proud Hollywood Star Lanes, where *The Big
Lebowksi* was filmed, and the four private lanes in
the VIP section consistently host high-rollers.

101 COFFEE SHOP

6145 Franklin Ave., Hollywood (323.467.1175)

Boozy Hollywood club kids sober up at this old-
school diner, complete with a glittery acoustic
ceiling and faux wood laminate countertops, for
late-night burgers, pancakes, and omelets—just as
Vince Vaughn's Trent did with his posse in the 1996
movie *Swingers*. The crew eats lunch at this greasy
spoon—located just off the 101 Freeway and inside a
Best Western hotel.

EPISODE 5: The Script and the Sherpa

GOLD'S GYM

1016 Cole Ave., West Hollywood (323.462.7012)

While many patrons at this muscle mecca may look like they just stepped out of an Abercrombie ad, most
people come here to pump, not pose. Vince takes a yoga class here with his vegan squeeze, Fiona, who insists
the boys guzzle down shots of wheatgrass juice (tasty!). Later, a nude Josh Weinstein slips
Eric the *Queens Boulevard* script in the locker room.

REAL FOOD DAILY

414 N. La Cienega Blvd., West Hollywood (310.289.9910)

Rabbits rejoice! A restaurant dedicated to the eating habits of our furry
little friends. All right, maybe that's an exaggeration, but at this PETA-
approved, all-organic eatery, there's nothing made with animal or dairy,
cholesterol, eggs, fats, sugars, or refined flours—which may be real
good for your body, but not for your agent. "I'm on Atkins," Ari says
when he meets Vince, Fiona, and the guys there. "I need protein, real
protein, like man protein, from the flesh of slaughtered animals." What,
no salisbury seitan?

MASTRO'S STEAKHOUSE

246 N. Canon Dr., Beverly Hills (310.888.8782)

Mastro's is clearly an *Entourage* favorite. Vince tries to convince *Queens Boulevard* producer Scott Wick that he's the real deal at this ritzy establishment with its deep dark mahogany walls and dim lighting, where upper-level industry execs, agents, and actors come to both press and eat flesh. Ari takes the guys here in Season 3, Episode 3 to toast *Aquaman's* success, and is lured back by Babs, who suckers him into a meeting with the heads of the top talent agencies (who invited APA?) in Season 3, Episode 8.

EPISODE 6: Busey and the Beach

PINK'S

709 N. La Brea Ave., West Hollywood (323.931.4223)

At this classic hot-dog stand, Eric gets a call from Ari about Lakers tickets. Patrons who love Pink's understand patience; the lines are always down the block, but the amazing dogs, chili, and fries make it worth the wait.

TOPANGA STATE BEACH

18700 Pacific Coast Highway, Malibu

Park your car in the lot. Lay out on a towel. Pretend to read a magazine as you really check out smoking-hot chicks in bikinis. And for Christ's sake, watch out for Gary Busey.

EPISODE 7: The Scene

THE COFFEE BEAN & TEA LEAF®

7235 Beverly Blvd., West Hollywood (323.934.1449)

No, Ari, it's the Coffee Bean & Tea Leaf®, not the Starbucks across the street. A-listers often amble by this California chain's WeHo location after shopping at Kitson or Lisa Klein on Robertson. It's also where Ari set up a makeshift office after his Jerry Maguire-style departure from the agency in Season 2. You just can't overestimate the appeal of their caffeinated concoctions.

CHATEAU MARMONT

8221 W. Sunset Blvd., West Hollywood (323.656.1010)

Hollywood's Chateau Marmont, perched high on a hill above the famed Sunset Strip, has long been a beacon of discretion—making it the perfect place to misbehave. So it's no surprise that it's the place where the boys first meet *Queens Boulevard* director Billy Walsh, enjoying, like many before him, a booze-and-babe-fueled bender in the hotel's penthouse suite, which will set you back $3,500 a night.

TOAST BAKERY CAFE

8221 W. 3rd St., West Hollywood (323.655.5018)

Transplanted New Yorkers, twenty-something scenesters, industry up-and-comers, and established actors flock to this low-key bakery/café, especially for weekend brunch, packing the tiny tables set up on the sidewalk. The guys rap about Vince's going-away party here, and again take a table in Season 2, Episode 13, when the boys tell Vince that Mandy Moore is stepping out on him with her former fiancé, but he refuses to believe it.

TABLE 8

7661 Melrose Ave., West Hollywood (323.782.8258)

Wanting to become his full-time manager, Eric invites Vince to this cozy, upscale California seasonal restaurant (located on a busy block beneath a tattoo parlor) to "wine and dine" him—in other words, convince him that they need to formalize their working relationship, but Vince is all about the status quo. The heated conversation ends with E storming out of the place, which has served countless actors and lists comedian Jamie Kennedy as an investor.

167

season 2
Entourage hotspots

EPISODE 1: The Boys Are Back in Town

THE APPLE STORE

1248 Third Street Promenade, Santa Monica
(310.576.1011)

Doug Ellin is a self-professed "die-hard Mac person" (even Ari uses an iMac), so it's no surprise that Turtle would bribe a clerk at the Santa Monica Apple Store with a signed *Head On* DVD so that Drama would be selected to model at the iPhoto seminar, thus saving him two grand on headshots. Turtle's back two episodes later, shamelessly trying to return swag Vince received so he can get some cash and buy cashmere pajamas for the party at the Playboy Mansion. Sadly, all he can get his hands on is a store credit.

EPISODE 2: My Maserati Does 185

VAN CLEEF & ARPELS

300 N. Rodeo Dr., Beverly Hills (310.276.1161)

If pirates ever invade Beverly Hills, they would surely ransack Van Cleef & Arpels, one of the finest—and priciest—jewelry stores in the world (and they have the stone-faced security guards to prove it). E buys Kristen $1,400 worth of "guilt jewelry" here after he cheats on her. Later, Kristen admits her own indiscretions and Eric kicks her to the curb, returns the jewelry, and walks out with the blond salesgirl's digits. Vince buys his mom an entire display case for the *Aquaman* premiere in Season 3, Episode 1.

THE PENINSULA BEVERLY HILLS

9882 S. Santa Monica Blvd., Beverly Hills (310.551.2888)

Back from New York, Eric had planned a romantic evening with Kristen at what many consider to be Beverly Hills's best hotel. This beautiful French-Renaissance property offers ninety-six lavish guest rooms, a stunning rooftop pool and spa, and even a Rolls-Royce service to chauffeur guests around town in style. But when Kristen feigns food poisoning and cancels, he ends up taking the Perfect 10 model he met at Jaime Pressly's party here instead. While the Peninsula's exterior was shot for the show, set designers recreated the hotel room on a soundstage.

BARNEYS NEW YORK

9570 Wilshire Blvd., Beverly Hills (310.276.4400)

This ultra-luxe store is the place for the rich and famous to buy designer duds (think Lanvin and Balenciaga) in Beverly Hills. The guys stop by the third floor men's department to pick up fancy PJs for Hugh Hefner's big bash. Turtle, tuck in those tags!

I CUGINI

1501 Ocean Ave., Santa Monica (310.451.4595)

The fab four meet Marvin the accountant at this Santa Monica Italian restaurant, which specializes in fresh seafood and offers outdoor seating with views of the Pacific Ocean, to discuss real estate. Unless he does a big studio movie, Vince has $1 million to buy a house. Not liking what he can get in his price range, he ends up dropping $4 million on Marlon Brando's old pad, which makes an *Aqua* check all the more appealing.

THE PLAYBOY MANSION

10236 Charing Cross Rd., Holmby Hills

The Mansion gets mentioned a few times in previous episodes before the boys finally stop by to live the centerfold dream with Hef at his legendary Holmby Hills bunny ranch, where Drama finally figures out who set those monkeys free. Damn that Pauly Shore.

PACIFIC DESIGN CENTER

8687 Melrose Ave., West Hollywood (310.657.0800)

Looking to furnish his new manse, Vince flops on a sleek modern couch at Menzie International, one of the 130 showrooms offering furniture, textiles, and other home items at the Pacific Design Center, a beautiful blue monolith located on a fourteen-acre campus. In addition to its many showrooms, the PDC houses an outpost for the Museum of Contemporary Art, two Wolfgang Puck restaurants, and a 380-seat theater.

EPISODE 5: Neighbors

PANE E VINO

8265 Beverly Blvd., West Hollywood (323.651.4600)

While the dining room at this Italian trattoria offers comfortable booths, the walled patio garden is definitely the place to see and be seen. The boys grab an outdoor table here after rapping with actor Anthony Anderson, who helped Drama get a gig in *Barbershop* (but, of course, his scenes were snipped). Hoping to end Turtle's dry spell with the ladies, Drama invites his "sure thing" to meet them, but as soon as she gets a whiff of Turtle's desperation, she bounces out the back exit.

170

4100 BAR

4100 W. Sunset Blvd., Silver Lake (323.666.4460)

This hipster watering hole located across the street from a Jiffy Lube in L.A.'s gritty-turned-hip Silver Lake neighborhood might look chic with its massive Buddha statue, black booths, and hanging tapestries, but it still maintains its rough edges and has the clientele to prove it. Standing at the red oblong bar, Eric tries to convince Billy Walsh to screen *Queens Boulevard* for James Cameron before it plays at Sundance. After another "no way, suit" speech, Walsh splits with a prostitute and E downs a shot of Jack.

EPISODE 6: Chinatown

CIRCUS DISCO

6655 Santa Monica Blvd., Hollywood (323.462.1291)

This cavernous gay nightclub can host more than 3,000 people and is often rented out for special events, such as EA's "Fight Night" tournament. A weed-free Turtle, boxing as the legendary Rocky Marciano, gets his ass handed to him in the first round by a cocky little ankle biter with some fresh dance moves. Ari braves boys' night at Circus in Season 3, Episode 14 to rescue Lloyd from TV writer Jay Lester.

EB GAMES

1000 Universal Studios Blvd., Universal City (818.980.5746)

Turtle test-drives a $250 controller at this store, located just outside Universal Studios theme park, while training for EA's "Fight Night" video game tournament.

PARK CITY

Park City is a bit of a sleepy town for eleven months of the year, but when the Sundance Film Festival comes, this remote mountain hamlet in Utah, 700 miles from Hollywood, entertainment industry chaos rules. Thousands of established and aspiring filmmakers, celebrities, agents, marketers, fans, and, yes, even entourages, flood the quaint streets day and night. Vince pulls on a parka to catch the debut of *Queens Boulevard*, a scenario that *Entourage* writer and executive producer Rob Weiss can relate to: His 1993 film *Amongst Friends* played the festival.

171

EPISODE 8: Oh, Mandy

VICEROY HOTEL

1819 Ocean Ave., Santa Monica (310.260.7500)

Near the pair of pools and private curtained cabanas at this boutique beachside hotel (which recently underwent a $15 million renovation), Ari hands Vince two envelopes: the first contains a check for two million "little fishies" for signing on to *Aquaman*; the other, James Cameron's short list of his female costars, which includes his former flame and *Walk to Remember* costar Mandy Moore. Fans of *The Sopranos* should also recognize the Viceroy as the spot where Christopher tries to pitch his screenplay to Sir Ben Kingsley.

HOWS TRANCAS MARKET

30745 Pacific Coast Highway, Malibu (310.457.0305)

While posting up at Jessica Alba's surfside mansion, the guys navigate the PCH to this MILF-packed local market, where Drama distracts Dr. Joyce Brothers with his "I wake up fully tented" line so Turtle can steal the last box of Froot Loops from her cart. Way to keep it classy, guys.

DRAGO

2628 Wilshire Blvd., Santa Monica (310.828.1585)

No, this place isn't named after Dolph Lundgren's Soviet super boxer from *Rocky IV* (but wouldn't it be cool if it was?). The guys roll the Escalade to this elegant Italian eatery and burn a jay in the car while Vince meets up with Mandy to see if they can put the past in the past and work together again. When she tells Vince that she's engaged to be married in a month, he asks E to get her off the film.

EPISODE 9: I Love You Too

172

SAN DIEGO

San Diego, located 120 miles south of Los Angeles, is best known as a Navy town. But it still has enough cool cache to draw the boys. After all, **Del Mar Thoroughbred Club** (where the boys go in Season 3) is just north of San Diego and is a classic racetrack founded by Bing Crosby that has pulled celebs since the Rat Pack days. Why wouldn't the gang want to kick it on the track's Don Julio Veranda Café and knock back tequila while the ponies do their thing? **Comic-Con**, the uber-geeky comics-and-more convention that draws more than 100,000 fans, was another reason the boys headed to "America's Finest City," as SD likes to call itself. For once, Drama got to be the star of the show, as fans gave him the cry of "Victory!"

THE BEVERLY HILTON

9876 Wilshire Blvd., Beverly Hills (310.274.7777)

Ari drops some serious coin on his daughter's bat mitzvah, held in one of the ballrooms of this enormous 570-room hotel, which is owned by Merv Griffin and hosts both the Golden Globes as well as the annual Oscar nominee luncheon.

EPISODE 11: Blue Balls Lagoon

JERRY'S FAMOUS DELI

8701 Beverly Blvd., West Hollywood (310.289.1811)

"This is Jerry's, not the Ivy," Vince says to E as they walk into this popular but decidedly low-key Beverly Hills delicatessen (which offers a menu that reads like *War and Peace*, with more than 600 items) to meet Mandy Moore. E's worried that the press will spot Vince and Mandy together after Page Six ran an item about their rekindled romance. "You see any paparazzi here?" Vince asks. Well, you just might, as many stars have been known to dine at Jerry's.

173

LUCQUES

8474 Melrose Ave., West Hollywood (323.655.6277)

While sipping fireside cocktails at this West Hollywood hotspot renowned for its romantic atmosphere and delicious Cal-French fare, Eric learns more about Sloan and her velvet hammer of a father, Terrance, who "is great with all weapons" and "even better with his bare knuckles."

MULBERRY STREET PIZZA

240 S. Beverly Dr., Beverly Hills (310.247.8100)

The boys lament the lack of good pizza in Los Angeles (it's the water) at the start of Season 2, but Mulberry Street's thin-crust NYC-style masterpieces are the exception to this rule. Named after a street in Little Italy, Mulberry was opened by *Raging Bull* star Cathy Moriarty, and often becomes so packed with hungry customers that a twenty-minutes-at-a-table time limit goes into effect. Vince and Turtle chow down on some slices here in Episode 19 and wonder if an angry E will come to Mandy's birthday party.

EPISODE 13: Exodus

CARTIER

370 N. Rodeo Dr., Beverly Hills (310.275.4272)

After E earns a $200,000 commission from repping Vince on *Aquaman,* he agrees to share the wealth and buy Turtle and Drama gold watches at Cartier. When they walk out, they spot Mandy and Chris leaving Gucci across the street and decide to tail her (in the sizzling yellow Hummer no less) to see if she's cheating on Vince. "That's what happens at Gucci," Drama says. "Buy a pair of shoes and they let you fuck your ex-fiancé."

174

HAMBURGER HAMLET

9201 W. Sunset Blvd., West Hollywood (310.278.4924)

Tsetse fly! Unable to work for an increasingly hostile Terrance (who has announced his plans to return full-time), Ari puts his plan for a putsch into effect and holds a top-secret meeting with the other defecting agents at this upscale burger chain because "Nobody who works in this business would ever be caught eating there," he says. Too bad no one else shows up. Ironically, the Miller Gold Agency is forged here in Season 3, Episode 8 when Babs comes to the rescue after Terrance refuses to pay Ari's $11 million settlement.

THE LITTLE DOOR ➜

8164 W. 3rd St., West Hollywood (323.951.1210)

Yes, the door to this fantastic French-Mediterranean restaurant is little (it's a good way to spot this place from the street, as it doesn't have a sign). Sloan offers to help Eric find a job with her father here. Reservations are a must, and if you're fabulous enough to make the list, the little door opens to a private canopied patio where the pretty people, young and old, smoke, drink, and look lovingly at each other while munching on mussels. Or you can opt for an indoor table, which are strewn with rose petals. We're not kidding.

FLOYD'S BARBER SHOP

7300 Melrose Ave., West Hollywood (323.965.7600)

Floyd's is the kind of old-school joint where they still use shaving cream and straight razors to clean up what's cooking on the back of your neck, but it's also new-school enough to have punk-rock posters on the walls and offer free Internet access. Turtle stops by the Melrose store (there's also one on Santa Monica Boulevard) to talk to the shampoo girl, who knows Dr. Dre, about Saigon's upcoming musical showcase.

KIEHL'S

100 N. Robertson Blvd., Beverly Hills (310.860.0028)

Celebrities just love Kiehl's body, skin, and hair-care products because it makes them all soft, silky, and shiny. Budding music manager Turtle says he sent word to Damon Dash about Saigon's performance while in this store.

EPISODE 1: Aquamom

MICHAEL KORS

360 N. Rodeo Dr., Beverly Hills (310.777.8862)

In anticipation of Mrs. Chase's arrival in L.A. for the *Aquaman* premiere, Vince, along with Eric, Shauna, and Christy, attempts to transform her from bridge-and-tunnel to red-carpet ready at this famous designer's boutique. Excited to see his mom, Vince decides to buy a whole rack of dresses in different sizes. "Does that make me a pussy?" he asks Shauna. "No, it makes you man," she replies, "and a very handsome one."

PRO ITALIA MOTORCYCLES

3319 N. Verdugo Rd., Glendale (818.249.5707)

When *Aquaman's* opening-weekend box-office numbers crest eight figures and begin to close in on Spidey's record, the guys celebrate at this Ducati dealership, where Vince buys four of the fastest production bikes on the road, even though Drama "is a Harley man" but had to sell his hog to Michael Madsen after a slow pilot season.

EPISODE 3: Dominated

SPIDER CLUB

1737 N. Vine St., Hollywood (323.462.8900)

Tucked above the supper club Avalon, this exclusive Hollywood hangout is housed in the same building where the Beatles made their first West Coast appearance in 1964 (before they played the Hollywood Bowl). The boys take the recently released, sex-starved fifth wheel known as Dom to this Moroccan-themed lounge, where the *US Weekly* set is known to kick back among the Persian rugs and pillows and swing from the in-house dancing pole.

SIX FLAGS MAGIC MOUNTAIN

26101 Magic Mountain Parkway, Valencia (661.255.4100)

This enormous theme park's famous roller coaster, "Goliath," which climbs twenty-six stories and then drops 255 feet while reaching speeds in excess of 85 miles per hour, doubled as "Aquaman The Ride," which Vince is there to promote in this episode.

ERMENEGILDO ZEGNA

301 N. Rodeo Dr., Beverly Hills (310.247.8827)

Dom finally gets a shirt with some sleeves at this high-end Italian designer's Beverly Hills boutique and weighs in about Vince having to travel up to Santa Barbara to charm *Medellin* producer Phil Rubenstein when he has several other multimillion-dollar offers.

JACK N' JILL'S

342 N. Beverly Dr., Beverly Hills (310.247.4500)

Try the country-fried steak sandwich or the chocolate-chip-and-pecan pancakes at this light and airy down-home-style eatery, where Vince and E interrogate the Dominator, asking if he stole the Shrek doll from Phil Rubenstein's house.

O'GARA COACH COMPANY

8833 & 8845 W. Olympic Blvd., Beverly Hills (310.659.4691)

After *Aquaman* beats Spidey's opening-weekend record, Vince rewards his own "super friends" with matching convertible Aston Martin roadsters. Turtle gets an extra bonus at this dealership, which also sells Bentleys, when Vince tells him that the Power 106 DJ is going to play one of Saigon's tracks on air.

SPAGO

176 N. Canon Dr., Beverly Hills (310.385.0880)

Spago—the crown jewel of Wolfgang Puck's epicurean empire—is synonymous with white-tablecloth dining in Hollywood. Turtle and Drama set some land speed records when racing here for a power lunch with Ari (can you really call "shotgun" on a meeting?) and nearly bash bumpers trying to valet park. After some chitchat, a charitable Ari agrees to add both of them to his client list (Victory!). Vince and Amanda lunch here and act like they're in a "bad Meg Ryan movie," according to E, in Season 3, Episode 16.

THE PALM See page 163

ROOSEVELT HOTEL (also Dakota)

7000 Hollywood Blvd., Hollywood (323.466.7000)

The guys' night out gets pumped full of estrogen when they run into Sloan by the pool at this historic Hollywood hotel, which hosted the first-ever Academy Awards back in 1929. E and Sloan come back here and grab a table at Dakota (the hotel's restaurant) with Tori for a pre-ménage cocktail. Later, in Season 3, Episode 7, Vince gets lucky in the Roosevelt's coatroom during Sloan's charity event.

BLOWFISH SUSHI

9229 W. Sunset Blvd., West Hollywood (310.887.3848)

Even ADD-afflicted diners nearly pass out from overstimulation at Blowfish, with its walls packed with flat-screen TVs that play Japanese anime accompanied by a blaring techno track. The imaginative rolls of raw fish are pretty damn awesome. After meeting Alan Grey here, Ari walks out front and calls Vince to tell him that the studio head agreed to $10 million for *A2*.

LA SCALA

434 N. Canon Dr., Beverly Hills (310.275.0579)

E and Sloan work out the rules of engagement for their threesome with Tori at this refined Italian restaurant, known for its chopped salad. When making a reservation, remember to request one of the crescent-shaped red vinyl booths and ask about the chicken Parmesan. It's not on the menu, but it sure is delicious.

HUSTLER HOLLYWOOD

8920 W. Sunset Blvd., West Hollywood (310.860.9009)

As Eric gears up for this big night as the hypotenuse in a Sloan-and-Tori triangle, the guys discuss the finer points of a three-way in *Hustler* publisher Larry Flynt's X-rated emporium, which offers a veritable pornacopia of DVDs, novelties, latex toys, and lingerie. Oh yeah, it also has a fancy coffee bar.

IL CIELO

9018 Burton Way, Beverly Hills (310.276.9990)

After settling with Terrance to the tune of $11 million, Ari swings by this exquisite Italian restaurant, with its ceiling frescos, vine-shaded patios, and a hearty-yet-urbane menu that offers rose crème brulée with candied rose petals on a bed of white chocolate and raspberry sauce for dessert, to sweep a lunching Mrs. Ari off her feet with a diamond large enough to choke a baby.

EPISODE 8: The Release

DIALOG COFFEE

8766 Holloway Dr., West Hollywood (310.289.1630)

Before his audition with Eddie Burns, Drama's temper redlines at this West Hollywood coffee house and bakery when his tenth-purchase-for-free card is refused. Adding insult to injury, the Escalade gets towed while he's arguing with the manager over his latte. Good thing he didn't have his nunchakus with him.

LAS VEGAS

Vegas, baby, Vegas! What happens in Vegas stays in Vegas. Sin City. Glitter Gulch. The Entertainment Capital of the World. This desert den of debauchery a mere 270 miles away from L.A. is a second home to young Hollywood. From getting comped at the **Palms Hotel and Casino's** "Real World" Suite, to brawling with Seth Green in the **Hard Rock's Body English** nightclub, to getting paid great big piles of green for judging a stripper contest, the *Entourage* guys did Vegas their way.

180

EPISODE 10: I Wanna Be Sedated

BOOK SOUP

8818 W. Sunset Blvd., West Hollywood (310.659.3110)

Known for their floor-to-ceiling bookshelves, high-profile events, and celebrity clientele, Book Soup is the place in L.A. where the literati meet the glitterati. It's also a good spot to hook up—or it least it was for Vince, who meets a book-smart hottie in the magazine aisle, only to discover, post-coital, that she's engaged and he's on her "celebrity list," meaning that her fiancé is cool with her sleeping with Vince.

THE STANDARD HOLLYWOOD HOTEL

8300 W. Sunset Blvd., West Hollywood (323.650.9090)

No hotel in image-conscious L.A. is more calculated in its "coolness" than the Standard—with its hanging bubble swings, shag carpet, and beanbag chairs in the lobby—located smack dab in the middle of the bar-and-club-choked Sunset Strip. Drama gets an upside-down view of this modern hotel's blue Astroturf pool deck when he's hung over the balcony by Saigon's new manager's homeboys.

UNDEFEATED LA

112 S. La Brea Ave., West Hollywood (323.937.6077)

Vince refuses to play the celebrity card and cut in line when he and Turtle arrive at this supercool sneaker store so Turtle can spend some of his Saigon cash on a pair of limited edition Fukijamas. The two never make it inside, but if they did, they would have been welcomed into a shoe-lover's paradise, with hard-to-find kicks (Undefeated has collaborated with Nike on special issues of Air Force Ones and Dunks) displayed around a serene waterfall and reflecting pool.

UNDEFEATED SM

2654-B Main St., Santa Monica (310.399.4195)

Vince and Turtle rush across town to pick up one of the last remaining pairs of Fukijamas, only to discover that DJ AM snagged them minutes before they arrive. They may have had more luck if they would have drove east instead of west; Undefeated recently opened a store in Silver Lake in the Sunset Junction shopping district.

EPISODE 12: Sorry, Ari

LE PETIT FOUR

8654 W. Sunset Blvd., West Hollywood (310.652.3863)

Thanks to Lloyd and the gay assistant corps, Ari knows about Vince's meeting with a rival agent at this bustling French bistro, which offers patio seating, great food, and an unobstructed view of the smog parade down Sunset. E, Drama, and Turtle run into *Gotcha!* host Pauly Shore here in Season 3, Episode 16.

EPISODE 13: Less Than 30

IL FORNAIO

301 N. Beverly Dr., Beverly Hills (310.550.8330)

Months after Vince and E break up with Ari over the Ramones snafu, they agree to meet him for a "just friends" lunch full of awkward silence at this Northern Italian eatery famous for its rotisserie-style chicken, fresh-baked bread, and modern-but-homey décor.

QUEEN MARY

1126 Queens Highway, Long Beach (562.435.3511)

Turtle goes a little overboard throwing Vince's Victoria's-Secret-sponsored birthday bash on this historic luxury ocean liner (now permanently docked in Long Beach as a tourist attraction and hotel) that once played travel host to Hollywood stars and was even used to transport troops in WWII.

PRANA CAFE

650 N. La Cienega Blvd., West Hollywood (310.360.0551)

Couples' weekend up in Napa becomes a question mark when Eric asks Vince to find a date-worthy girl to bring up to the wine country as the two sit on the sidewalk patio of this cozy café, which serves scrumptious American and Pan-Asian dishes and welcomes dogs, so long as they're with their owners.

THE GRILL ON THE ALLEY

9560 Dayton Way, Beverly Hills (310.276.0615)

If you can score a booth here, you're at the top of Hollywood's food chain. The Grill on the Alley is where the town's true power players come to power lunch. Ari takes Lloyd with him here to sign syndication king Jay Lester, the famous TV writer. What happened to working with actors, Ari? "Fuck actors," he says. "Too much heartache."

184

REPUBLIC RESTAURANT + LOUNGE

650 N. La Cienega Blvd., West Hollywood (310.360.7070)

Located on a stretch of La Cienega called "dining row," this ritzy new restaurant's menu offers contemporary American dishes infused with a bit of southern flair, as well as an extensive wine list. Eric and Sloan go on a double date here with Vince and Lindsay the coatroom girl. Sloan and Lindsay end up hitting it off, thwarting E's plans for a romantic weekend without Vince.

JAR

8225 Beverly Blvd., West Hollywood (323.655.6566)

Forget the horses and British accents. Vince and E meet a "frustrated" Amanda at this 1950s-style supper club that serves comfort meats like pot roast and Kansas City steaks to let her know that it's a no go on the Edith Wharton/Sam Mendes project. Vince also tells her she's "cute" and ends up giving her more than just a piece of his mind.

EPISODE 16: Gotcha!

LE PETIT FOUR See page 183 & **SPAGO** See page 177

EPISODE 17: The Return of the King

See **SAN DIEGO**, page 172

NORMS

470 N. La Cienega Blvd., West Hollywood (310.657.8333)

Drama and Turtle find King the horse (and the cops) in the parking lot of this nostalgia-inspiring L.A. coffee shop, where you can still get a decent cup of joe and a T-bone steak for less than what you'd pay to park your car at most local places.

EPISODE 18: The Resurrection

CUT

9500 Wilshire Blvd., Beverly Hills (310.276.8500)

Wolfgang Puck's newest steak house, with its minimalist modern interior, white-oak floors and multiple skylights, is one of the hardest reservations to get in town, and that's because the place serves a damn good cut of beef. E, Vince, and Ari lunch with *Matterhorn* producer Joe Roberts here to see if he'll pony up the cash for *Medellin*.

EPISODE 19: The Prince's Bride

ANTONIO'S

7470 Melrose Ave., West Hollywood (323.658.9060)

Turtle and Kelly escape her father's watchful glare at this mellow Mexican restaurant located in the heart of the Melrose shopping district. While you might be tempted to order a beer to go with your authentic, stick-to-your-ribs meal, know that Antonio's fully-stocked bar also offers private-label wines and tequila.

BEVERLY WILSHIRE HOTEL

9500 Wilshire Blvd., Beverly Hills (310.275.5200)

How badly does Vince want the money to make *Medellin*? Not enough to pimp himself out to former Ukrainian soap star Nika Marx when they meet at the glamorous Beverly Wilshire Hotel—where *Pretty Woman* was filmed—even though Vince admits having "a thing for Eastern Bloc women."

EPISODE 20: Adios Amigos

THE GROVE

189 The Grove Dr., West Hollywood (323.900.8080)

Shauna calls Drama while pushing a stroller by the circular fountain at this outdoor shopping mall (adjacent to the historic Farmer's Market) that's made to look like an idealized small-town Main Street. She tells him that he can't rent an $800-a-month studio apartment because "Vincent Chase's brother cannot be living like a transient crack whore."

MONDRIAN HOTEL

8440 W. Sunset Blvd., West Hollywood (323.650.8999)

Located on the Sunset Strip, the Mondrian is called "the hotel in the clouds" because of the stunning southern views from literally every room. Vince and company decamp here after selling the mansion and later raise a glass on the balcony together before heading off to Bogotá.

ENTOURAGE GLOSSARY a users guide

aquamanify /verb/ to make something grossly commercial; what Billy Walsh won't let the studio do to *Queens Boulevard.*

ass patrol /noun/ scouring the clubs and events for hot chicks to bring home for the after party; a duty that usually belongs to Turtle.

bat phone /noun/ Ari's emergency cell phone that he reserves the right to answer—even during therapy.

Black Hack /noun/ the gang's illegal connection to everything from weed, to "whisper quiet" G-5 planes, to mortgages, to clean urine.

bomb /noun/ a movie that fails at the box office, or Eric's worst nightmare for Vince and Ari's worst nightmare in general.

boom /verb/ a signature Ari expression, said with staccato emphasis, to indicate that he has taken care of business and the deal is done.

break-up sex /noun/ a last act of intercourse between a couple that's aware that their relationship is over; Eric describes **break-up sex** as "afterward you say goodbye." Drama observes this is thus "the only kind of sex I have."

Brian's Song /noun/ ultimate "guy-cry" movie; how Drama and Turtle figure out that Mandy was cheating on Vince with her former fiancé, Chris.

'Bu /noun/ short for Malibu, an upscale beach colony northwest of Los Angeles, where the guys stay in Jessica Alba's waterfront pad.

bubble kush /noun/ the type of weed that Rufus has stashed in the wheel well of his Deville.

Chiang Chung /noun/ the hottest director in Hong Kong who shot his "Wire Fu"–influenced commercial for an energy drink that gave Vince $500,000 for one day's work.

cock block /verb/ to obstruct a man's game with a female when he's trying to get laid. E accuses Vince of trying to **cock block** his date with Emily.

crip weed /noun/ the best smoke the Hack has to offer; known to enhance your video game playing skills.

crossing swords /verb/ when two penises accidentally touch during a threesome. "It's no biggie," Turtle says after his Sundance ménage. "It's an occupational hazard."

cruelty-free lifestyle /noun/ what vegan Fiona lives, meaning that she won't eat or wear anything that's killed. However, as Ari explains: "Even broccoli screams when you rip it from the ground."

D-girl /noun/ abbreviation for "development girl," a lowly position in the studio hierarchy that was once filled by women almost exclusively. Ari calls Dana

Gordon this to belittle her even though she's an executive at Warner Bros.

Dongka Donka /noun/ Fiona's "channel name" according to the Sherpa.

drunk dial /verb/ to call someone when you're all boozed up and feeling desperate, needy, and/or horny. What E does when he mistakenly calls Kristen instead of Emily and leaves a message for the wrong girl.

E-bola /noun/ Dom's nickname for E, calling him an "infectious fucking disease," which E really hates.

fall-out pussy /noun/ the leftover ladies that a TV/movie star will leave for his friends, as Drama explains, referring to his "*Melrose Place* fall-out pussy" that the guys enjoyed when they first came to L.A.

fly-over states /noun/ The states between California and New York, a.k.a Middle America, where *Aquaman* must do well in order to guarantee its overall success.

Fukijamas /noun/ limited-edition Nike shoes named after the famous graffiti artist. Only 200 pairs are made and then they destroy the pattern.

fully tented /adjective/ sporting a boner in your boxers. Drama explains to Dr. Joyce Brothers that he wakes up this way. "Well, at your age, consider yourself lucky," she says.

Gay Assistants Corps /noun/ a secret society of homosexual assistants that all share information with each other; how Lloyd knows what's happening in Hollywood.

green room /noun/ a plush waiting room where the actors hang out before going onstage at a talk show like *Jimmy Kimmel Live*. Also where Ari tries to poach clients.

the head /noun/ a theory about famous folks from Turtle; the bigger the star, the bigger the head, as in Vince has got the talent and he's got the head. Drama, he's just got huge ears.

hip pocket /verb/ agent term for picking up a client informally, like Adam Davies did with Drama.

hundie /noun/ slang for $100, as in, "E, I need a hundie, bro. This girl's gonna jerk me in the back."

Illegally Blonde /noun/ Drama's nickname for actress Ali Larter, Vince's angry ex.

juggling the speed bags /verb/ fondling a woman's "chesticles," as described by Turtle.

liquid gold /noun/ Drama's name for Rogaine.

loop /verb/ to replace dialogue after the shoot as Vince does for *Queens Boulevard*.

Lucky Charm /noun/ another nickname for E.

mangina /noun/ what Vince's *Aquaman* action figure has between his plastic legs.

The Mansion /noun/ an abbreviation for Hugh Hefner's Playboy Mansion; also a place that Drama is temporarily banned from.

MILF /noun/ an acronym for "Mother I'd Like to Fuck"; Vince gets accosted by one who "wants to take him home" in the supermarket in Malibu.

M.O.W. /noun/ stands for Movie of the Week, a staple of Drama's acting career. And if it's made by Hallmark, this means Emmy.

no-fly zone /noun/ an area between Vince's waist and thighs. If a girl enters that airspace, "she's going down," he says.

non-closer /noun/ a person who can't seal the deal sexually; what the guys accuse E of being.

off book /adverb/ an actor giving his/her lines in rehearsal without a script; what Drama hopes to do with Brooke Shields.

P.C.H. /noun/ Pacific Coast Highway, how you get to Malibu from L.A. Where Drama experiences his golf-club road rage.

Pepperoni U /noun/ where Ari asks E if he went to school.

pre-interview /noun/ what actors give to producers so the host has talking points when they are live; what the *Kimmel* producers attempt to do with Vince's people.

pull a Chapelle /verb/ reference to comedian Dave Chapelle, who unexpectedly quit his successful Comedy Central show. Ari assures Alan Gray at Warner Bros. that Vince won't do this to the *Aquaman* franchise.

Pure Tour /noun/ the name of pop singer Justine Chapin's music tour.

Pussy Patrol /noun/ a comic book by porn star Jesse Jane and her girls who "lick ass by day and kick ass by night."

Q-rating /noun/ a scientific ranking of a celebrity's popularity used by the advertising, marketing and public relations industries. For example, Vince would have a much higher Q-rating than Drama.

revenge fuck /verb/ getting back at your ex-girlfriend by banging someone who looks exactly like her, as prescribed by Turtle to E after he and Kristen break up.

Robert Nitsche /noun/ Mandy Moore's favorite artist.

roofie her up /*slang*/ the only way that Ari can understand how E was able to hook up with a Perfect 10 model—by slipping her the "date-rape" drug Rohypnol.

Sbarro /*noun*/ East coast Italian restaurant chain where E used to be a manager, hence his nickname, "Pizza Boy."

Storm /*noun*/ *Aquaman's* animatronic seahorse.

suit /*noun*/ Billy Walsh's derogatory way of describing noncreative people. E is also known as "Supersuit."

suit approval /*noun*/ what Vince demands for his *Aquaman* costume so he doesn't end up embarrassed.

Tarvold /*noun*/ Drama's character on *Viking Quest*, who hails from Northumbria, not Orkney. ("Damn you, Turtle.")

top tall /*adjective*/ a description that Drama uses to critique women: "Torso's too long. Legs are too short. She was inverted."

the trades /*noun*/ referring to *Variety* and *The Hollywood Reporter*, two daily "trade publications" that cover the entertainment industry and are a must-read for anyone who works in showbiz.

tsetse fly /*noun*/ code phrase to start Ari's agency coup; also a reference to a line in the famous 1979 comedy *The In-Laws* starring Alan Arkin and Peter Falk.

Victory! Tarvold's famous *Viking Quest* battle cry.

war room /*noun*/ It's really just Ari's conference room at the agency, but, as Lloyd says, calling it that "makes him feel like a gladiator."

west-coast mother /*noun*/ how Shauna describes her relationship with Vince.

ACKNOWLEDGMENTS AND CREDITS

Entourage would like to thank Mike Askin, Ally Musika, and Kenny Neibart, with special thanks to Lisa Alden.

HBO would like thank Stacey Abiraj, Chris Albrecht, Bree Conover, James Costos, Amy Gravitt, Nona Jones, Gurmeet Kaur, Eric Kessler, Jamaal Lesane, Mara Mikialian, Jada Miranda, Courteney F. Monroe, Tonya Owens, and Carolyn Strauss.

Melcher Media would like to thank Pocket Books, especially Margaret Clark and Anthony Ziccardi, Kim Bello, Sophie Bonsor, Nicholas Cope, David E. Brown, Sue Hostetler, John Hughes, Nancy King, Amelia de la Mora, Lauren Nathan, Clive Piercy, Alessandra Rafferty, Dominick Ricci, Lia Ronnen, Rusty Sena, Ellen Sitkin, Rhonda Spies, Lindsey Stanberry, Alex Tart, Peter Christiansen Valli, Betty Wong, and Megan Worman. Special thanks to Stephen Saito for his help writing the Episode Guides. And thank you to the entire cast and crew of *Entourage* who helped to make this book, especially Susan Paley Abramson, Mike Davis, Chase Harlan, Roemehl Hawkins, Tim Schulz, and Amy Westcott.

IN MEMORIUM/DEDICATION:
Bruno Kirby, Chris Penn, and Stanley DeSantis.

192

Photography All photos by Claudette Barius/HBO except for the following: 1-7: Courtesy of HBO (opening credits); 13: (top) Courtesy of Bruce Mars, (bottom): Courtesy of Doug Ellin; 22-23: Courtesy of HBO (opening credits); 30-31: Nicholas Cope/HBO; 32-33: Mark Seliger; 42-43: Nicholas Cope/HBO; 49: Mark Seliger; 51: Courtesy of HBO; 52-53: Nicholas Cope/HBO; 59 (top): Nathan Sayers/HBO, (bottom) Nicholas Cope/HBO; 60-61: Nicholas Cope/HBO; 68: (bottom) Ron Batzdorff/HBO; 69: (center) Ron Batzdorff/HBO; 72-73: Courtesy of HBO (opening credits); 74: (Queens Boulevard press kit) photographed by Nathan Sayers/HBO; 75: Courtesy of HBO; 82-83: Nicholas Cope/HBO; 84 (bottom): Courtesy of Chase Harlan; 90-91: Ron Batzdorff/HBO; 99: Masaru Uchida/Amana Images/Getty Images; 100-101: Nicholas Cope/HBO; 108: (top right) Ron Batzdorff/HBO; 109: (clockwise from top) Mastheads Courtesy of *The Hollywood Reporter*, Courtesy of American Media, Inc., Courtesy of NYP Holdings, Inc., Courtesy of Reed Business Information, a division of Reed Elsevier Inc.; 122: (Artie Lange) Courtesy of Doug Ellin; 125: Doug Hyun/HBO; 126-127: Courtesy of HBO (opening credits); 128: ("Sloan") Ron Batzdorff/HBO; 131: (bottom right) Doug Hyun/HBO; 142: ("Nick Rubenstein") Doug Hyun/HBO; 150: Doug Hyun/HBO; 151: (from top to bottom) Courtesy of Bentley Motors, Inc., Courtesy of Maserati North America, Inc., Courtesy of Ford Motor Company (Land Rover), Courtesy of General Motors Corporation (Cadillac) (The CADILLAC and HUMMER EMBLEMS are trademarks of General Motors Corporation. While General Motors has granted authority to the author of this book to display the CADILLAC and HUMMER EMBLEMS, General Motors does not endorse or assume any responsibility for this publication, the technical accuracy of its contents, or the opinions expressed therein.), Courtesy of Hyundai Motor America, Courtesy of Mercedes-Benz USA, LLC, Courtesy of Mercedes-Benz USA, LLC (Maybach), Courtesy of Ford Motor Company (Aston Martin), Courtesy of General Motors Corporation (HUMMER) (same credit as previous General Motors Corporation entry), Courtesy of American Honda Motor Co., Inc., Courtesy of Ducati, Courtesy of Ford Motor Company (Lincoln), Courtesy of Rolls-Royce Motor Cars NA,LLC, Courtesy of BMW North America, LLC; 152: (car) Courtesy of Mercedes-Benz USA, LLC; 153: (clockwise from top) Courtesy of Mercedes-Benz USA, LLC, Getty Images/Newscom, Courtesy of Bentley Motors, Inc.; 155: (Hollywood Hills) Peter Christiansen Valli (image from *Hip Hollywood Homes*); 162: (top) Courtesy of Arclight Hollywood, (bottom) Courtesy of Koi; 163: (top) Nicholas Cope/HBO, (bottom) Courtesy of STAPLES Center; 164: (top) Courtesy of Lucky Strike Lanes, (bottom) Courtesy of RFD, Inc; 165: (top) Courtesy of Pink's Famous Hot Dogs, (bottom) Courtesy of The Coffee Bean & Tea Leaf®; 166: Courtesy of the Chateau Marmont; 167: (top) Courtesy of Toast Bakery Café, Inc, (bottom) Courtesy of Table 8; 168: Nicholas Cope/HBO; 169: Courtesy of Playboy Enterprises, Inc; 170: Courtesy of Pane e Vino; 171 (bottom): Nicholas Cope/HBO; 172 (bottom right): Courtesy of Del Mar Thoroughbred Club; 173: Nicholas Cope/HBO; 175: (top) Nicholas Cope/HBO, (bottom) Courtesy of Kim Reierson; 176: Courtesy of Spider Club; 177: Courtesy of O'Gara Coach Company, Beverly Hills' authorized factory dealership of Aston Martin, Bentley, Bugatti, Lamborghini, Rolls-Royce, and Spyker; 178: Courtesy of La Scala; 180: (bottom): Courtesy of Charles Day; 181: Nicholas Cope/HBO; 182: Courtesy of Undefeated, Inc; 183: ©RMS Foundation/The Queen Mary; 184: (top) Courtesy of Prana Café/Divine Dining, Inc, (bottom) Courtesy of Republic Restaurant + Lounge/ Divine Dining, Inc; 185: Courtesy of Norms; 186: Doug Hyun/HBO; 187: Courtesy of Morgans Hotel Group.

Illustration/Artwork 76-77: Courtesy of Ph.D; 85: Courtesy of Ph.D; 93: Courtesy of Ph.D; 109: Prop Artwork Courtesy of HBO; 159: Felix Sockwell; 160–161: Courtesy of PH.D.

Entertainment journalist and book author Tim Swanson has been chronicling the collision of art and commerce in Hollywood for more than a decade. He holds a B.A. in English and Spanish literature from Willamette University and a Master's in journalism from the University of California at Berkeley. Swanson lives in Los Angeles with his wife Anita and their two dogs.

For 20 years, Santa Monica studio Ph.D has been involved in design and communications for clients such as Nike, Peerless Lighting, Herman Miller, Chronicle Books and Roxy/Quiksilver. Design: John Hughes and Clive Piercy. www.phdla.com

This book was produced by:
Melcher Media, Inc.
124 West 13th Street
New York, NY 10011
www.melcher.com

Publisher: Charles Melcher
Associate Publisher: Bonnie Eldon
Editor in Chief: Duncan Bock
Editor and Project Manager: Holly Rothman
Assistant Editor: Shoshana Thaler
Editorial Assistant: Daniel del Valle
Production Director: Kurt Andrews

ENTOURAGE, Seasons 1–3, Available on DVD from HBO Video.